Lawless River

Mack Johnson, if indeed that was his name, rode into El Paso having crossed the Rio Grande on a stolen horse. Was he a lawman, a professional gunfighter, a rustler or what? His past might be in doubt but he was certainly a mighty tough *hombre* who soon became the ruthless ramrod of the largest property owner in town.

The future looked good for Mack but then it all started to go wrong. First information about his past began to emerge and then there was a power struggle in town.

He had never been in such a tight spot before and it looked doubtful whether, despite his remarkable skills with a gun, his plausibility and his charismatic appeal to women, he could be saved from the hang rope.

Lawless River

Jake Martin

A Black Horse Western

ROBERT HALE · LONDON

Robert Hale Limited
Clerkenwell House
Clerkenwell Green
London EC1R 0HT

Typeset by
Derek Doyle & Associates, Liverpool.
Printed and bound in Great Britain by
Antony Rowe Limited, Wiltshire

CHAPTER ONE

The horse was lathered, its eyes glaring, foam blowing like white sea-spume from the corners of its mouth. The rider leaned low over its neck as if to push it to greater speed. If the horse faltered in its stride he quirted it savagely. The straining creature lurched over the rocky uneven floor of the pass. On both sides of them rose rock-formations, sometimes sheer like walls, sometimes sloping away and leaping upwards in fantastic crags and outcrops.

The floor of the pass began to rise and the horse slackened its pace and blew gustily. The rider quirted it again, with no perceptible result. The beast could not make another ounce of speed. The man let his quirt fall to the side of his trousered leg, smack against the high-heeled riding boot. He was hunched in the saddle, his ten-gallon hat low to shade his face from the glare of the now slowly-dying sun.

The rock-floor became smoother, and the weary horse kept lurching and sliding. The man jerked again and again at the reins with little petulant gestures. He pulled too hard and suddenly the beast reared, its back feet slipping, the hoofs ringing. It gave an almost human cry of pure terror and its four legs seemed to give way at once. The man threw himself clear as the horse keeled over on its side.

The rider stood away from it, panting. The horse twitched then lay still. Its eyes rolled upwards piteously. Its leg was broken. The man moved in, drew his gun with a quick gesture, pointed it at the beast's head. Then he became tense, the gun still pointed. He did not press the trigger. He held the gun there and only his head moved as he looked about him. He was alone in the pass, the rocks all around him and, at the far end, the mouth of the pass, a glimpse of shining green: the range he had left behind him.

With the same swift gesture he holstered the gun, turned his head away from the horse's imploring eyes. But those eyes were on him as he unlashed his bedroll, took his rifle from the saddle-boot. He turned away then and began to climb the rock. He kept climbing until he was gasping for breath, his legs like rubber, sweat streaming down his face. His bedroll hung on his back; he carried his rifle in one hand and climbed with the other, changing hands from time to time. He stopped and looked downwards. The pass was a ribbon, the horse a dot in its centre.

From time to time he looked down and the pass seemed narrower, the dot smaller. He could also see that glimmering green patch of range, and he kept looking until suddenly that was blocked out and he knew that he had no time to pause and look any

6

more but had to keep climbing. He glanced upwards where the rocks soared away from him, pocked and lumpy like the sloping terrain of a strange new world. The crest of his endeavour still seemed miles away.

His face, strained upwards, was unshaven, sweat glistening on the reddish-dark hair. It was a young face, a strong face with a desperate wolfishness about it. For a moment the sun gave it a red, almost devil-ish look, then the shadows took over and the glow moved upwards, tinting the rocks above. Red, copper, gold – and the man strove desperately, a creature seeking the sun, a fly pin-pointed on a slop-ing wall of rock. Looking again he saw the flash of green once more. He saw the cluster of dots moving away from it, moving along the now-darkening pass like bugs on a dirty ribbon. He saw the other still dot in the centre of the pass then, when he looked again, all the dots were mingling together.

The shot was a flat thin sound; the echoes billowed around him then died away in the rocks above. Clinging to a knob of rock with one hand he watched the dots beginning to separate again but the larger bunch moved more slowly, and were spread out as if seeking.

Once again the climber strove to reach the crest above. Then, after all, he was there. He lay on his stomach, his body shook as great gasps burst from it.

After a little while he wriggled around and peeped over the edge, down the steep bumpy slope. It seemed so easy now. So easy that they could all climb it and reach him quickly.

He wriggled backwards from the edge; kept on

wriggling, despite bruises and scratches, until he was sure he could not be seen from below. Then he rose to his knees. He remained like that, his head bent, his back bowed beneath the weight of the bedroll, his rifle lying on the ground beside him. After a moment he grabbed the rifle, rose to his feet and started forward.

He stumbled over the uneven ground in his scuffed high-heeled boots, skirting huge fantastic outcrops of rock, boulders as big as houses, misshapen leafless trees sprouting at all angles.

After a few hundred yards of this the ground became more even and began to slope downwards, and he was looking out across the mesa, short-cropped grass interspersed by patches of sand, all tinted by the dying rays of a blood-red sun.

As far as the eye could see there was nothing but the semi-barren plain. No shelter; no habitation, or beckoning glade or valley, or glint of water amid green. The man pushed his hat back from his eyes and his shoulders drooped tiredly.

He hitched the bedroll from his back and tucked it under his arm. Then, with the rifle swinging in his other hand, he began to walk again, his hat pulled over his eyes, his head bent, blindly. The ground danced before him and quite suddenly he came upon the flat beaten path. He raised his head and looked around him. He stood on a trail, which he realized must run parallel with the gulch. A small boulder was close beside him. He sank down upon it, lifted the fringe of his bandanna and wiped his face. He was sweating from exertion but already the sun had died, the shadows were gathering and he knew the night would be cold up on this flat top of the world. Looking along the trail to where it thinned and finally vanished, he saw what appeared like a brown pug of smoke. It grew larger as he watched it, blossoming, growing fringes at the edges. As it grew so the man's hopes grew with it until he was sure that the thing he watched was not smoke but dust from the wheels of a fast-moving wagon, from thundering hoofs.

From his shirt-pocket he took a sack of 'makings'. He rolled himself a cigarette, lit it, and sat smoking and watching the rapidly spreading dust cloud. Finally he could see that it came from a covered wagon drawn by a team of four horses. They looked good horses and the wagon was new and shining, travelling swiftly and smoothly.

There was only one man on the box-seat up front, a straight, broad old man, whose white hair curled strongly from under a battered slouch hat.

The young man rose, cigarette dangling from his lips, and walked to the middle of the trail with hand uplifted. The old-timer slackened the horses' pace; his eyes were sharp as he looked downwards. Then something about the other's pose, the wild unshaven look of him, mirrored danger. He shrieked at his horses and cracked his whip across their backs. They bounded forward; the wagon rocked at crazy speed.

Standing there, the young man crouched and went for his gun. But he was not quick enough: the horses bore down on him and he had to throw himself desperately aside. He rolled and his gun hit the dust a few yards in front of him.

He rose, lurched to the rock and picked up his rifle. Then he ran away from the trail until he could see the galloping horses clearly, though their driver was hidden from him by the white canopy of the wagon.

The young man dropped to one knee and cradled the rifle against his cheek. The rifle barrel moved slowly in a half-circle as he followed the passage of the galloping horses with his sights. He squeezed the trigger.

One of the rear horses pitched sideways. The one before it swerved, dragging the carcase behind it, then stumbled. The wagon rocked crazily then crashed over on its side. The old man flung himself from the box, rolled, and lay still. Two of the horses broke free and galloped on madly. The other one rose to its feet and stood trembling beside the body of its dead companion. The dust billowed and drifted and settled.

The young man picked up his bedroll, picked up his gun and holstered it. He swung the bedroll on to his back and, with the rifle held ready for action, moved swiftly forward. There was that hungry wolfishness about his face again.

He went to the wagon, ran a practised eye over the trembling, unharmed horse still caught fast between the shafts, then he climbed into the wagon. After a few seconds he got down and walked across to the old man once more and lifted him. He staggered beneath the weight and it seemed he tried not to look at the bloodied face as he carried the limp form.

He placed it in the wagon then got down. He took up his bedroll from beside the trail and unrolled the blanket. He folded it neatly into a square. He went to the beast in the traces and placed the improvised saddle on its back. Though he gentled the horse with his hands, no sound came from between his set, stretched lips.

Unhitching the horse he led him to the side of he trail. He picked up his rifle and the small bundle which had been rolled in his blanket. He mounted and urged the horse forward. They went slowly at first then, as beast and rider gained confidence in each other, at ever-increasing speed.

He did not look back. The wagon and the dead horse remained forlorn on the desolate plain.

CHAPTER TWO

The sun was sinking like a huge gout of blood when they had their first sight of the river, which itself seemed like a sluggish stream of blood, glowing sullenly against the deepening night-haze rising behind it.

The Rio Grande, the famous river; the divide between states, across whose waters revolutions had been fought. It had run with blood and the blood had gone sour. It did not look like the gates to the 'Promised Land', but to the weary lobo on the tired horse it was. He hit the horse on the rump with his clenched fist, for his quirt was back in the pass and he had no spurs, and urged the beast into the sluggish waters, yellow now, as if with corruption.

The animal snorted and tried to back away from this cold biting thing. The man kicked it then, leaning forward on its neck as if he was hissing imprecations into its ear. The startled beast plunged, almost went under, then began to swim desperately. The man held his rifle above his head with one hand but disregarded the bundle in front of him.

The current was stronger than it looked, there was an insistent insidiousness about it, an evil pressure that almost had the horse over once or twice. Pieces of brushwood floated by, twisting and turning, grotesque debris from a dead world.

The first signs of real life were on the other bank, trees angling out over the water. As they approached the other side, the horse almost succumbed to the sucking current; the rider grasped an overhanging bough, steadying the beast with knees tightly pressed to flanks. Slowly they reached firm ground and the horse stood panting and shivering.

The man looked about him in the pink-grey twilight, noting now that the trees were sparse and bare. He turned the horse's head to the right and urged him forward once more. His face was out-thrust and predatory in the half-light. There was still a hungry urgency about him.

The horse cocked up its ears as the sound of a train whistle came faintly from the distance. As they went on there was no more sound except the muffled drum of hoofs, and the faint soughing of a slowly-rising night-breeze.

Darkness fell suddenly, as if a blanket had been draped across the sky. A slowly rippling blanket which hid the moon and the stars. The wind began to moan and the first drops of rain plummeted down. It was pouring in sheets when they finally saw the lights of the town, pale flashes in the shimmering haze.

El Paso Street was a river of mud when they passed along it, the horse weary and limping, the man like a sodden rag on its back. The rain ran in streams in the cart-ruts; the thoroughfare was empty, but lights blazed from most of the windows along the first part of its length. The rain in the ruts was turned by the garish yellow lights into miniature rivers of silver.

There was a hum over the town like a giant, pulsing turbine, the hum of many voices. At frequent intervals the hum was broken – by shouts, by laughter, a snatch of song, the clankety-clank of a piano. This was El Paso, the 'wide-open town', with the hodge-podge of a dozen nationalities, the stamping-ground of gamblers and gunmen, cowboys and teamsters, pimps and prostitutes, confidence men, pick-pockets, sneak-thieves – and other human scum for whom no label could be found.

The rider found a livery-stable, prised the fat Mexican proprietor away from a whiskey bottle, and extracted a promise from him that he would take good care of the horse – and his rifle and stuff too. There was something about the savage insistence of this sodden, unshaven man that made the proprietor promise readily and watch his departing back with something like relief.

The lean young man went along the boardwalk, beneath the shelter of the awning, beneath the soaring gimcrack false-fronts. He passed the wooden steps of a gaudy theatre, one of El Paso's proudest acquisitions since the 'boom', and a woman swathed in a blanket-coat leered at him from the paybox.

'Come on in, cowboy,' she called. 'The show's only just started.'

He ignored her. Water dripped from him, but he seemed to have lost his tiredness. His scuffed heels went slap-slap on the boardwalk with a triumphant sound. He turned sharply a few yards past the theatre and went through the swinging doors of a large brilliantly-lit honky-tonk.

Folks eyed the dripping figure curiously as he stood on the threshold, then they turned away. Just another saddle tramp! The women wore plenty of frills and laces and the men broadcloth and fancy vests. It was a fancy place.

The young man shook the rain from him, took off his hat and slapped it against his thigh. Some drops spattered a gambler who sat at a table with his back to him. The gambler turned, scowling, an angry remark rising to his lips. Something he saw in the other's face checked his tongue. He shrugged as if in disgust and turned away.

Swinging his hat in his hand the young man worked his way through the throng. All around him were 'sporting' tables on which every conceivable game of chance could be played. Faro; Three-card Monte; Poker; Hazard, or its speeded-up equivalent, Craps; Roulette; Chuck-a-Luck; Banco; Thimble-rig . . . Most of the tables and lay-outs were presided over by poker-faced, cold-eyed members of the ironically-titled 'sporting gentry'. On a high-stool against the bar sat the 'look-out', a tall, thin, pale-faced young feller decorated with crossed gunbelts and wicked-looking guns to match. From his perch he could overlook the whole of the room and go into action if any trouble started.

A cigarette dangled from the corner of his mouth and, with fish-like eyes, he watched the dirty, sodden stranger as he advanced. The latter bellied up to the bar a few yards away from the look-out and did not even glance in his direction. The thin man swivelled a little on his stool and continued to watch him.

The bartender was burly, black-jowled. He eyed

the stranger from under thick jutting brows.

'Rye,' said the man hoarsely. 'A big one.'

The barman said: 'You'll hafta check in your gun, *amigo*, before you drink here.'

The other's hand dropped to his belt. 'My gun?'

'Yeh. It's one o' the marshal's new rules.'

'Yeh . . . ? Stop spoutin' an' give me that rye.'

'Sorry, *amigo*. Nobody here's wearin' a gun. I don't make the rules.'

'What's the matter with El Paso? It used to be "wide open".'

'Still is, where everythin' else is concerned. But there's a no-gun rule in all these establishments. The proprietors find it better for them if they back the marshal in that respeck. Leastways, that's what my boss says.'

'Give him the gun, *amigo*,' said a soft voice behind the stranger.

The man turned his head slowly, the wolfishness about him more pronounced than ever. The barman watched him warily, his arms dangling below the bar. The thin man had gotten down from his stool and, thumbs hooked in crossed belts, stood beside the stranger.

The latter's eyes smouldered. '*You're* wearing guns.'

'I work here. Hand it over, *amigo*.'

'Maybe you'd like to try an' take it.'

'I could do that,' said the look-out. He stepped back a few paces.

Attention was now being drawn to the incident. People watched, but moved back in doing so.

The stranger's dark eyes seemed to smoulder. The thin man in front of him watched the killer light blos-

16

som there like a dull flickering flame. Then, as quick as it came, it had died. The eyes were dull and blank again, tired.

The man turned away, drew his gun slowly, reached out to put it on the bar. The look-out either misconstrued his motion or did not mean to let the quarrel die. He went for his guns.

The stranger still had his hand on the butt of his gun; he swung it swiftly, spinning on his heels. The barrel hit the side of the look-out's head with a dull smack. The man went over; his gun went off, the slug bringing a shower of plaster from the ceiling. Before he hit the floor the stranger was turning, covering the bartender.

'Bring those hands above the bar – an' make sure they're empty.'

The burly man raised them slowly. The stranger moved further along the bar. Then suddenly he vaulted it. He moved up alongside the bartender and stooped a little. He came up with a sawn-off shotgun and placed it on the bar out of the man's reach. His hot eyes surveyed the room.

'You all saw that,' he said. 'I was handing in my gun when that thin bozo tried to jump me.'

Nobody answered him right off. The vapid, vicious and shifty faces looked up at him. Then a voice from the midst of them said: 'Stay right where you are, young fellah.'

The young man watched, like an animal at bay, as the ranks parted and a man came through. He was tall, and wore a suit of rusty broadcloth and a battered hat. A huge silver watch-chain was draped across his vest and above it, no less shiny, was a star. His face was mahogany-coloured and decorated by a luxuriant black moustache. In one brown fist was a huge Colt .48. It did not look too big for him.

The two guns faced each other, the man behind the bar drew back his lips in a snarl.

'Stay where you are,' he said.

The marshal halted. He said: 'If that's the way you want it, son, it's just a matter o' shootin' it out. That way it's quite probable we'll both be killed. If you kill me somebody else is sure to get yuh. Then again I might kill you first an' only be wounded myself. If you're a gaming man like most of my friends here you must realize that all the odds are on my side. I ain't askin' yuh to back down like a yeller dawg, I'm just askin' yuh to be sensible an' place your gun on the bar there.'

The level voice died and there was dead silence, a silence vibrating with tension. The two men faced each other, their eyes boring into each other, their guns levelled. The snarl had died from the young man's thin lips. He looked a little uncertain – still like an animal at bay. All he had to do was press the trigger – show his hand. Could he be sure how the cards were stacked against him? Whether the lawman was popular with this crowd, or hated like so many of his kind in these hell-spots of the West?

The look-out lay and bled on the floor between them.

It seemed like there was only he and the marshal in the room, in the whole wide world. He did not see the barman move slightly beside him. Not until the burly man sprang did he turn swiftly: and then it was

18

too late: a rock-hard fist smote him on the side of the head. As he was staggering, striving to keep balance, to steady his gun and turn it, another blow hit him in the side. As he fell a boot jarred harshly, agonisingly on his upper arm and he dropped the gun.

The boot swung again and missed him. He rolled, grabbing at the swinging leg; he missed it. The barman used both feet, putting the boot to his man, in time-honoured way, with cruel finesse. Another savage kick at his shoulder sent the stranger down again. The barman was aiming for his head, to put him out for good. The shadows below the bar got darker as the marshal suddenly landed on his feet there.

'Cut it, Sam,' he yelled.

The heavy boot swung impotently then came to rest with a bang on the floor.

'On your feet, young fellah,' said the marshal. 'You're under arrest.'

The young man rose slowly, his hand on the bar-top. His eyes were dull now but there was a taut sense of waiting about him.

The marshal stepped back a little, warily, his gun levelled. 'Out o' the way, Sam.'

As his voice died another echoed sharply. 'Run him out of town, boys. Teach him that it wouldn't be wise to come back.'

Men started from the crowd, advanced towards the bar. Behind them, shepherding them, came a little man with a little pinched face, a black broadcloth suit that seemed too large for him, a huge grey cravat at his scrawny throat.

'I don't want no-goods in my place.' The high-pitched voice came from him again, yet was like an echo, seemed to bear no relation to him.

The marshal turned his head slightly, still keeping his eyes warily on the stranger. 'Since when don't you want no-goods in your place, Luke?'

'Smart,' said the little man. 'Smart.' He gave a spurt of high laughter. 'Look at Phil. That no-good might've killed him.'

The 'look-out' was rising to his feet, staring around him owlishly, wiping blood from his face.

'He asked for it,' said the stranger suddenly. 'He drew on me while I wasn't looking.'

One of the men from the advancing band helped Phil to his feet. The thin man groped for his guns.

'Hold it,' barked the marshal. 'Get back, the whole damn' bunch of yuh. Make way. Call your dogs off, Luke, an' don't act the goat.'

'He's their meat, marshal.'

'Call 'em off I say. I'm the one who has the gun out. Seems to me your pet sharpshooter ain't in no condition to argue.' He jerked a thumb at the swaying Phil. 'Do you want I should shoot some of your dogs, Luke?'

'Heaven forbid,' said the little man. His high voice had a sardonic ring – amusement, mockery? it was hard to say.

'Get over the bar, young fellah,' said the marshal.

His eyes on the men before him, the stranger did as he was told. There were about half-a-dozen of them, maybe more behind, they were like dogs, sniffing towards a bone, each one leary of making the first movement.

The marshal sheathed his gun and, in the same movement, grabbed the barman's shotgun.

'Get back,' he said. 'Before I make rag dolls outa the lot of you!'

'All right, men,' said little Luke. 'Let the officer an' his prisoner come by.'

As the marshal got over the bar, another man came out of the crowd. Another man who looked like a gambler. Pale smooth face, moustache and side-burns, dark grey broadcloth, flowered vest, gold watchchain and huge fob. This character said: 'It happened just like the young man said, marshal. He was handing his gun to the barman when Phil drew on him. Phil would have killed him if he hadn't acted like he did.'

'It's a lie,' said Phil, whiningly, his hand pressed to his head.

'He asked Phil if he'd like to take it,' said another voice.

A general clamour of voices rose. The audience looked fair to be splitting into two factions.

'Anybody want to lay any bets?' said a wag at the back.

Little Luke turned on the newcomer. 'What are you doing here, Apgood? I don't want any Gruber men in here. Go poke your nose someplace else.'

'I'm slumming,' was the suave reply.

Luke's plug-uglies began to look tough again. The smooth-faced man backed away and disappeared into the crowd in the wake of the marshal and his prisoner.

As the two men passed through the swing-doors two others joined them.

'My deputies,' said the black moustached man casually. 'This is Pete – this is Charlie.'

21

Neither the deputies nor the prisoner bothered to greet each other.

'I'm Marshal Steve Maginnis,' went on the other imperturbably. If that name made any impression on the stranger he did not show it. Maybe he had heard of Steve Maginnis. But maybe he hadn't known that Maginnis had recently been made law-officer-in-chief of El Paso. Maybe he knew; maybe he didn't. Maybe it didn't make any impression either way.

The quartet went along the boardwalk, in shelter, the rain slashing past them, the street like a shining-stream surging by. They passed the theatre, they passed other honky-tonks, gin-mills, *bagnios*; and hole-and-corner places which did everything, and defied description.

Finally they reached the little 'dobe jail and the marshal unlocked the door and one of his men went in front of them and lit the lamp in the little office.

The marshal tossed him a bunch of keys. 'Take him through,' he said.

The deputy drew his gun. 'Come on, pardner.' He shepherded the stranger through an iron-studded door into the jail-block. Plank floor, swinging lamp already lit, but dim, running out of oil, four cells like cages along one side, a blank wall the other.

The light did not penetrate far into the cells and the deputy shut the stranger in the end one. In the semi-darkness he saw the faint glow of the small high barred window, the bunk against it, nothing else. He stood at the gate of the cell, rolled himself a cigarette, and lit up. Then, with this stuck in the corner of his mouth, puffing jerkily, he began to pace.

He was still pacing half-an-hour later when the deputy came into the passage, refilled the lamp and turned it up. The illumination showed the unshaven face as it became still at the barred gate. The eyes seemed to glare in the light, the face was that of a human wolf.

The deputy was a little startled. He said truculently: 'What's the matter with you?'

'Can a man get a cup of coffee an' somep'n to eat?'

'Whadyuh think this is – the mission-house?'

'Cut the lip – go tell your boss I want to see him.'

The deputy cursed but he went. He returned about fifteen minutes later with a cup of coffee and some corn biscuits on a tray. He put the tray on the floor in the middle of the passage and drew his gun.

'Get back,' he said. 'Right back against the wall.'

Something like a grin creased the other man's dirty unshaven face. He backed and sat down on the bunk.

The deputy bent and pushed the tray along the floor with one hand. He pushed it right under the cell-door, the cup scraped the bottom. He straightened up and holstered his gun. He said: 'Shove it back when you've finished with it.'

'What's the marshal keeping me here for? He can't hold me for anything.'

'Can't he? He says a night in jail 'ull do you good. In the morning I guess you'll either be run outa town on a rail – or jest lynched.'

'Which do you favour, pardner?'

The deputy merely spat.

'Where's yuh boss?'

'He'll see you in the mawnin'.'

23

CHAPTER THREE

The marshal unlocked the door and went right into the cell. The prisoner, who sat on the bench smoking, watched him. The morning sunshine spotlighted the lawman's moustached, mahogany face, but the prisoner was in the shadows. His cigarette glowed, he was motionless.

'What's your name, son?'

'Johnson – Mack Johnson.'

'Where'd you come from?'

'No place in particular. Jest ridin'.'

'This town's full o' folks who come from no place in particular and are just ridin'.'

'So? Do you ask all of 'em a lot of fool questions.'

'If they behave themselves, I don't.'

'I didn't come here lookin' for trouble. That thin lookout bozo started it.'

'Yeh, so you said. Which way did you ride in last night?'

'Along the river.'

'Where from?'

'Came from the Pecos, was in Cripple Rapids yesterday.'

'Stay there long? Get to know anybody there?'

'Nope, was only there a day.'

'Left your hoss in Pueblo's livery, didn't you?'

'Fat greaser?'

'Yes.'

'Yeh, that's where I left it.'

'The beast was mighty wet.'

'It'd bin raining mighty hard, hadn't it. You'd expect him to he wet.'

'Him? It's a mare.'

'I allus call hosses *him*. That mare's got more guts than a stallion anyway.'

'You got a saddle?'

'No. I lost it in a crap game at Cripple Rapids. Didn't bother to get one 'fore I left.'

'The mare was all muddy. Almost as if she'd forded the river.'

'She blundered into the edge of it in the rain.'

'Yes, it was like hell, wasn't it?' said the marshal with a sudden change of tone.

He took a gun out of his belt and handed it across, muzzle foremost.

'There's your iron. You're free. But I'm warning yuh, if you aim to stop in El Paso you've got to behave yourself. Don't wear your iron in the dives at nights – an' keep out of the *The Golden Hall* altogether.

'*The Golden Hall*?'

'That's the place you were in last night. Luke Piercy's boys have put the eye on you, they'd welcome a chance to chew your ears off.'

Mack Johnson rose and stretched himself. His eyes were red-rimmed in his dirty face.

'You did a hell of a lot of pacing last night,' said the marshal.

'I can't sleep in a strange bed.'

'If you're on the run, I don't want anybody catchin' up with you here.'

'I ain't on the run.'

The marshal shrugged, turned towards the door. Over his shoulder he said: 'There's a pump out back if you want to wash up. There's a cake o' soap there, too, I guess.'

'Thanks.' Mack Johnson's voice was flat, unenthusiastic.

He followed the marshal out. The latter pointed. 'Use the back door . . . So-long.'

'So-long,' said Johnson.

The door closed behind him. The marshal turned and regarded the blank wood for a moment as if he expected to see questions and answers written upon it. Then he combed his luxuriant moustache with his fingers and went on down the passage to his office.

Outside, Mack Johnson peeled off his leather vest, his dirty shirt and his even dirtier red flannel under-vest. He found some soap in the gutter beneath the pump, sluiced himself then made a thin lather with the yellow stuff. His body was lean, muscular, pretty hairless compared with his face. The muscles across his shoulders were pock-marked with what looked like old wounds.

He washed himself thoroughly, his long dark-reddish hair as well, and wiped himself on his shirt. He did not put this on afterwards but donned his

leather vest, buttoned up tightly, on top of the red
flannel.

The shirt he rolled up into a ball which he tucked
under his arm. He walked around to the front of the
jail and made his way along the boardwalk.

He went first to the livery-stable. The fat Mexican,
whom the marshal had called Pueblo, came from out
back rubbing his eyes and yawning. Already he smelt
of liquor, among other things.

'Where's my hoss?'

The Mexican blinked then recognized the man in
the half light.

'Eet ees here, *señore*. I take good care of eet.'

'Where is it?'

'Here, *señore*.'

The man led the way. He had spoken the truth.
The horse had been taken care of. Lazy though he
was, Pueblo loved his charges.

'Mighty fine beast,' he said.

'Yes,' said the man absently. It was a mare all right.
And he had known it all along. He cursed himself for
that slip of the tongue in the jail. It was forgotten
probably. But he shouldn't make slips like that – it
showed he was getting careless.

'You want the horse now, *señore*?'

'No, keep her here. Where's the nearest barber-
shop?'

'Jest 'cross the street.'

'Thanks.'

Mack Johnson minced out on his high-heeled
boots and his long shadow went before him. The fat
old Mexican watched him until he passed beneath

the barber's pole and into the gloom of the shop. There was a young man who could be a mighty bad *hombre* if he chose.

The barber looked up from lathering another customer and said: 'Mornin', suh.'

'Mornin',' grunted Mack Johnson.

He took the other vacant chair. He did not seem to notice that there were two other persons waiting their turn. They were staid shopkeepers, running to fat; they took one look at the rough-looking young man and held their peace. The barber shrugged slightly and flourished his razor.

The customer rose, wiping his face with the towel. Tall and straight in dark grey broadcloth, flowered vest, gold watch-chain with huge fob. The towel was dropped and Mack Johnson looked into the smooth, moustached face of the man who had intervened in *The Golden Hall* last night, the man whom Luke Piercy had called Apgood.

He smiled with a flash of white teeth. He was a goodlooking jasper. 'Good morning.'

'Mornin',' said Johnson.

'I trust you feel no worse for the inconvenience you suffered last night.'

'Bit sore. That's all.'

The tall man gave the barber a crumpled bill and made a slight motion of his hand when the man delved in his pocket for change.

'Thank you, Mr Apgood.'

'Good morning, all.' The tall man made a slight bow and walked from the shop. He moved like a cat.

'Haircut and shave,' Mack Johnson told the

barber. 'An' leave the moustache.'

'You're just growing one, suh.'

'Yeh, I'm just growin' one. Cut the gab and get on with it.'

'Yes, suh.'

There seemed to be a faint mocking smile on the face in the mirror, as if the man was laughing at this pip-squeak who would take lip from anybody in order to further his business.

Mack Johnson's hair was long, curling around his ears and into his neck. He said. 'Crop the mop short. Very short.'

'Yes, suh.' The barber flourished his scissors and began to slice at thick locks with alacrity.

Then minutes later Mack Johnson left the shop. Apart from his rumpled dirty clothes and the lean hard look of him he bore little resemblance to the young man who had gone in. Now that the black growth had gone his face did not look so dark. It was sallow and smooth. The moustache was bristly and black and the battered ten-gallon Stetson sat awkwardly on the cropped head. Mack Johnson looked little different to any wild harum-scarum cowboy. Not so lolloping maybe, a little more saturnine, a little more wolfish in his walk and watchful in his ways.

He looked about him as he walked, saw the tall man, Apgood, crossing the street towards him but did not pause in his stride. Apgood hit the boardwalk behind him, caught up, and fell into step with him. 'Feel better now?'

'Yeh.'

'I'd like to talk to you when you can spare the time.'

'Right now I've got business. Later uh?'

'All right. How about meeting me lunch-time?'

'Yeh.'

'See that hash-house over the street?'

'Yeh.'

'It don't look much but the food's good. Meet you there at twelve-thirty.'

'All right.'

'The name's Apgood. Jesse Apgood.'

'Johnson. Mack Johnson . . . See yu'n.'

Apgood took his dismissal and went. The mocking smile crossed Johnson's face again. But this time it was a little uncertain. He entered the place called *The El Paso Emporium* and was greeted by an obsequious man in a black wash-leather apron. Johnson said he wanted some duds.

He picked what he fancied from the varied stock, from the fanciest to the cheapest, hard-wearing. He went into a cubicle to change. Emerging, he looked like a new man. Handing the shopkeeper a bundle, he said, 'You can burn these.'

The sun was rising as he stepped out into the street. The dust danced from the boardwalk. It played tantalisingly on Mack's new outfit. His sombrero, Mexican-style, was black, and had a snake-skin band. His kerchief was red, his shirt pearl-grey; on top of it, swinging open, a fur-lined tooled leather vest. Black trousers, piped in red, and high-heeled fancy-top riding boots with Mexican-type rowels completed the outfit. The only incongruous thing was the greasy canvas body-belt and the sagging gun-belt which looped it, the shapeless holster, the gun with the scarred walnut butt.

At first glance this man could be taken for a Mexican. There were thousands of them in El Paso, they probably had more of a free hand here than in other American towns. They were on the whole a happy people, though superstitious and suspicious. There were bad ones, there were good ones.

Pueblo looked up as the man entered. He opened his mouth to call a greeting, but the words remained unspoken. He squinted in the half-light. This was no Mexican friend. Something eluded him.

'Trot my hoss out, *amigo*,' said the man and Pueblo remembered the voice.

He squinted again over his shoulder as he went to fetch the mare but he did not say anything.

Mack Johnson rolled himself a cigarette as he waited.

'You have saddle, *señore?*' said the Mexican as he brought the horse out, Johnson's rifle and bundle under his arm.

'Nope, I gotta go buy one. Can you recommend a place?'

'I've got some good ones right here, *señore*. My two beeg sons, they made them. Very fine saddles.'

'All right, let's look at 'em .'

Pueblo had not over-praised his wares. The saddles were good and strong and delicately tooled. His sons were, undeniably, craftsmen. Mack Johnson chose one and paid for it from a roll of bills he took from his body-belt. The roll was getting slimmer.

The saddle was complete with a rifle-boot. As Johnson mounted he stashed his rifle. Then he tossed the bundle to Pueblo.

31

'You can take care of that for me, *amigo*. I shan't be away long.'

'*Sí, señore.*'

As Johnson sent the horse out of the stables he saw Jesse Apgood on the other side of the street. The tall man was getting about quite a lot this morning. He did not seem to notice the horseman, who rode out of town, towards the Rio Grande.

CHAPTER FOUR

When he returned it was noon and the sun was at its zenith. It had dried the mud of the morning, and there were new patterns in the cart-rutted streets. The boardwalks were already just as dusty as usual.

Johnson passed the place of his rendezvous with Apgood. He did not see the tall man. He rode into Pueblo's place. The horse was muddy but showed no signs of fatigue.

The fat Mexican welcomed them with open arms, exclaiming again on the fineness of the beast. He was getting accustomed to the manner of its rider, who did not look so tough and disreputable now.

Johnson left Pueblo rubbing the horse down and went along the boardwalk towards the hash-house. A thin man approached him, passing across a bar of sunlight which revealed his pale face, his head swathed in bandages, the slouch hat sitting awkwardly atop them.

Their eyes met at the distance and the thin man's walk became springy; his face, in shadow now, seemed to go suddenly gaunt. His arms dangled but the fingers were curled upwards.

Mack Johnson did not slacken his pace. He was smoking. As he got nearer to Phil, he took the stub of the cigarette from his mouth and flipped it into the street with his left hand. Simultaneous with that movement Phil crouched. But he waited and that proved his undoing. His body tautened as he found himself covered by the stranger's gun. His own hands dropped to the butts of his guns and remained frozen there. He looked death in the eyes and his pale face went yellow, his milky eyes shifted so that he would not see the killer-light flaring in the eyes in front of him. His knees began to sag, words bubbled to his lips, but something held them there, unspoken. Then Mack Johnson spoke.

'I'm givin' you your last chance, friend. I might stay in this town for a while. I don't want you under my feet. Next time I'll kill you.'

Phil had been on the verge of pleading for his life. He could hardly believe his ears. As he stood there, his legs rocking, the other man holstered his gun, went past him without another look, and on.

Over his shoulder he said, 'Don't turn around. Walk on, the other way.'

Phil started to walk. After the first few steps his legs lost their rubbery feeling and began to tauten. Little prickles ran up and down his spine. That man was a killer: Phil had seen it in his eyes; he did not trust him.

Phil looked over his shoulder. The other man was still walking, his back straight. Phil whirled, drawing his guns, shouting, 'You! . . . You . . . !' inarticulately.

The man whirled. Phil grinned: the skunk could not make it. The grin died as something which felt like a spiked fist smote him high up in the side. As he went down, his ears were full of gunfire. Then everything exploded within him, and was gone. Dead!

Mack Johnson stood looking towards the still form. His gun was in his hand but it had not been fired. A window was open beside him, the window of the hash-house. Jesse Apgood leaned on the sill, leaned out, bareheaded, a smoking Colt in his fist.

'He was gonna shoot you as you turned,' he said. 'It's an old trick.'

'I know. I didn't think he'd have the guts. Thanks, *amigo.*'

'Forget it,' said Apgood. 'It'll teach you not to take such chances in El Paso.'

Behind him faces gathered, men came through the door of the hash-house. Two men ran from the other side of the street to the still form on the sidewalk. Apgood put a long leg through the window; his body followed, then his other leg: the way he did it seemed no more than normal. He joined Johnson on the sidewalk and the two of them went to swell the rapidly-growing, loudly-talking gesticulating bunch around Phil, the look-out.

An old-timer turned a whiskery face towards them, 'He's dead.'

'He ought to be,' said Apgood. 'I shot three times to make sure. I was in an awkward position you see.' He illustrated his meaning by raising a bent arm, as if he was still leaning on the window-ledge, and leaning sideways.

'I saw it,' said the old-timer. 'Phil tried to backshoot this young fellah.' He jerked a thumb at Johnson. 'On account o' what the young fellah did to him last night, I guess. Phil had it cumin' to him. Curly was with me – he saw it, too; didn't yuh, Curly? Hey, Curly

35

– where in tarnation air yuh? . . . There you air, yuh young skunk. Didn't it happen jest like I said?'

Curly was a tow-headed younker. He blushed as attention was turned towards him.

'Th – that's how it happened,' he said.

'I saw most of it from the window,' said another man. In elaborate detail he recounted the whole of it. The listeners hung on his words – until the disgruntled old-timer interrupted with: 'Aw, you see about everything that goes on in this town don'tcha, Sammy? There must be somep'n queer about you.'

'Whadyuh mean by that, you ol' buzzard?' Sammy started forward wrathfully.

The old-timer thrust out two fists, brown and gnarled and hairy like the rest of him, and advanced to meet him. Somebody caught hold of his arm and he shook it off with dignity.

'He thinks I'm too old. I'll show him.'

Members of the crowd got between the two would-be combatants. They milled and squabbled among themselves. The death of Phil, fallen so suddenly from the high perch he had occupied in the town so long – in *The Golden Hall* at least – looked like turning into a farce. He was forgotten, he was in danger of being trampled upon. He was dead; El Paso was a 'boom town': its business was with the living, and the farce was terminated by the sudden appearance of Marshal Maginnis and his two deputies.

The crowd parted to let them through. The marshal's keen dark eyes raked the faces around him. They came to rest on Johnson and Apgood, standing together, then they dropped. Charlie, the deputy, rose from his knees. 'Three slugs in the front of him,' he said. 'He couldn't be any deader.'

The marshal looked up again. 'Who did this?'

His eyes flickered at Johnson. There was a question in them.

'I did it,' said Apgood quickly.

Then Johnson was talking. 'He tried to shoot me in the back.'

'That's right,' cackled the old-timer suddenly. 'He'd've got him, too, if Apgood hadn't've shot when he did. I said to Curly I said—'

'Shut up, Zeke.'

'I was just trying to help, marshal.'

Other voices began to gabble. The voluble Sammy's and one or two more. The marshal turned to his deputies.

'Take the body to the undertaking parlour. Tell Sansome to leave it alone till I get there.'

'Sure, marshal.'

'Will you be all right with these hardcases? We oughta—' This was Charlie; the marshal interrupted him curtly.

'Go on.'

Charlie bent quickly and took Phil's legs. Pete, his pardner, scowled and with very bad grace, caught hold of the shoulders. The two men grunted in unison as they lifted.

They were not gentle with Phil. They bumped him against a wooden pillar then Pete cursed and dropped his head in the dust.

He glared at his pardner and said, 'Quit yuh shovin', will yuh?'

Charlie grinned. Pete lifted the head again and, followed by a troop of Mexican boys, they meandered on towards the undertaking parlour.

The marshal looked around him grimly. 'Johnson an' Apgood,' he said, 'I want you. An' Sammy, an' Zeke, an' Curly. Anybody else see what went on? *See* I said. Don't all speak at once.'

Finally he picked out two more men and led the whole party down to his office.

Fifteen minutes later Johnson and Apgood entered the hash-house and were bombarded with questions. The young stranger noted how most folks 'mistered' his companion and were diffident in their manner towards him. The tall man was 'somebody' it seemed. Questions were answered quickly – curtly. Another killing-case was closed. The marshal could not do anything else. Phil was no loss to the community anyway. He would be thrown into a hole in the ground in Boot Hill tomorrow or the day after.

'Mebbe Luke Piercy 'ull buy him a nice tombstone,' said somebody. 'He's bin a good servant to Luke.'

'Where is Luke?'

'He's outa town. Leastways, that's what I heerd.'

'He's gonna be hoppin' mad when he hears about this.'

'Let's get away from this rabble,' said Apgood. He found a table in a quiet corner. He ordered for both of them from an obsequious white-coated waiter. He looked about him, then he leaned across the table. 'I told the marshal I happened to be looking out of that window and I saw what Phil meant to do and knew I had to stop him. But that isn't the way it happened at all.'

38

'I figured it wasn't,' said Mack Johnson.

Apgood raised his eyebrows. 'Did you?' Then he smiled. It was white, flashing: it lit his face, but not his eyes.

'No, I saw you go by on the horse a bit earlier. Phil was on the other side of the street. He watched you – I guess you didn't see him.'

'I didn't.'

'He waited till you had gone in Pueblo's then he crossed the street. When he saw you come out he started to walk towards you. He was fast, Phil was, and he knew it. I guess you came as a surprise to him. Anybody else in town, knowing Phil as they do, would not have turned their backs on him. It was kind of fool-hardy.'

'You said somep'n like that once before.'

'Yes, I know, I shouldn't keep stressing the point. I'm sorry.'

'You don't hafta be sorry. You saved my life. All you gotta do is tell me why you did that?'

At this juncture the waiter came with the chow. Apgood smiled and kept on smiling, and waited until the man was out of earshot again. Then he said: 'You're very shrewd, Mr Johnson. You're nothing to me, you figure. Maybe not. But I like a man who can draw fast and has courage too.'

'That's a compliment I guess.'

'It is.'

'Thanks.'

'You're not very grateful to me for saving your life, are you?'

Mack Johnson did not answer this question. He

39

merely said: 'Put your cards on the table, *amigo.*'

'I'll do that eventually, Mr Johnson. I'm a gambler by profession and I like to play the game my own way.'

'I figured you for a gambler.'

'Is that a compliment?'

'Could be.'

After this interchange of smart talk both men bent over their plates. Apgood was the first to speak again. 'You aiming to stay long in El Paso, Mr Johnson?'

'I guess as you saved my life that gives you the right to ask me questions.'

'Suit yourself about answering them.' Apgood was the born gambler. There was no bile in his voice, his face was expressionless, his eyes flat.

'I aim to stay in El Paso some time. I ain't made up my mind for how long.'

'What are you aiming to do while you're staying here?'

'I hadn't thought much about that either.'

'Having something to do is better than frittering your time away, isn't it?'

'I guess so. Had you anything in mind that'd save me from getting bored in that way?'

'I'd like you to talk to a friend of mine. He might have a very interesting proposition to put before you.'

Mack Johnson did not say anything. His mind tried to grasp something. But the thing was elusive. It was just an echo. An echo of the voice of Luke Piercy, little owner of *The Golden Hall.*

Piercy, ordering Apgood out of his place last night, had mentioned somebody else's name, had called Apgood one of that somebody else's 'men'. The

40

name still eluded Johnson, but he knew now that Apgood, for all his airs and graces, was not the big boss in this shindig – whatever it was.

'I like meetin' people, so I'll meet your friend. If I don't like his proposition I'll say so.'

Apgood seemed in a hurry to be gone. He mopped his plate, gulped down the last dregs of his coffee. He called for the check. Mack Johnson let him pay it.

A few folks said 'So-long' to them, then they passed out into the afternoon sunshine. The El Paso dust was beginning to rise again, there were no signs now of the wet of the night before, nothing that spoke of the furious rain and the wind. The man who had ridden out of it, out of the night, and of the tumult of the Rio, had changed, too. He was handsome and well set-up and the girl who descended from the carriage, who nodded to Apgood's sweeping salute, gave him more than a passing glance.

He returned her glance boldly and turned his head and watched her as she walked across the sidewalk and through the doors of *The Golden Hall*. She had the largest bustle he had seen since he came to El Paso. A large bustle was a sign of affuence. She carried it well, too, and one lace-gloved hand held up her skirt a little so that a trim ankle was revealed as she walked. Her dress was blue satin, it shimmered in the sunshine, and atop it she wore a short red jacket affair, split at the bottom in the back to make way for the bustle.

She had a bosom, too, and a trim little waist, and her hair beneath the little hat was blue-black and long, sweeping down to her shoulders. He had caught a glimpse of her face and saw that it was very pale, cut like a cameo, with big dark eyes and full red lips to enhance its flawless beauty. Pale; with a haughty nod, not the frontier type at all. More like a French or Creole beauty. The sort you saw in New Orleans, the sort who took endless trips on the best-class river-boats. In many ways she matched the dandy who walked beside Johnson. And in other ways she did not. In some subtle way she had not looked quite so showy and cheap. But then, a man could not get a balanced viewpoint on a mere first glance.

CHAPTER FIVE

The carriage was black with gold designs on its door panels and around its window-cases, and brass scroll-work on the rail on top and at the boot. There was no luggage and the high-polished metal flashed in the sunlight. Through the window Johnson had gotten a glimpse of red velvet cushions.

High up on the box behind the four-team of magnificent black horses and, like them, seeming to be a fixed part of the equipage, was a huge negro. He wore a shiny top-hat and his livery was black and gold, highly polished. His ebony face shone as if that had been polished too.

He sat there immobile, staring straight in front of him. Some sixth sense seemed to tell him when the girl was safely inside *The Golden Hall* and with a smooth motion of his huge arm he flicked his whip and the horses moved off.

He drove them a little way forward then turned them slowly in the middle of the street. Then he whipped them into a canter. They sped past Johnson and Apgood in a cloud of dust which settled on these two lesser mortals as they went on their way.

The carriage was turning into a side-street as the

gambler led his companion into the theatre the latter had passed the night before, like a dog in the rain. The shutters were up and there was no leering woman in the paybox. The garishly decorated false-front looked rather cheap in the strong sunlight. The banner across it, which Johnson had not noticed before, flapped a little in the slight breeze. The young man read the words.

THE GREATEST SHOW IN THE WEST
THE GIRLS FROM PUITE BUTTES
SINGING AND DANCING IN A THREE ACT PLAY WHICH
WILL TEAR AT YOUR HEART STRINGS

Performances Twice Nightly

Johnson shrugged. Then he said, 'Who was the filly?'

'The filly?' Apgood's tone of surprise may have been genuine. 'Oh, you mean the young lady who went in *The Golden Hall.*'

'I didn't know there were any young ladies in El Paso.'

Johnson had a way of getting in a man's craw. But the poker-faced Apgood seemed very tractable. He gave another spurt of laughter and said: 'That was Louise Praline, she plays hostess there.'

'At *The Golden Hall?*'

'Yes.'

'What exactly does she do?'

'When they have a show she acts as mistress-of-ceremonies, she takes a hand at the tables sometimes – they say her eye can quell the toughest of the tough boys – she welcomes visiting celebrities.'

'What celebrities?'

'Now *you're* asking the questions, my friend. We had Wild Bill Hickok here last month. He wanted to take Louise with him – to deal faro in Austin—'

'An honour.'

'*She* didn't seem to think so.'

As he spoke Apgood had taken out a key and was unlocking an unobtrusive-looking little door beside the pay-box. He swung it open and stood aside to let his companion pass.

'Go ahead,' said Johnson.

Apgood gave a hardly perceptible shrug and walked before him into the gloom. The passage ran along the side of the auditorium. The walls were bare 'dobe, the floor bare boards upon which their boot-heels rang hollowly.

Suddenly Johnson flattened himself against the wall, his hand dropping to his gun.

'It's all right,' said Apgood. 'It's just one of the boys.'

The man who came out of the shadows was big and had a face like a not very intelligent ape. A gun dangled in his huge paw. He squinted at the two men, his little eyes almost vanishing beneath the overhanging brows of his low sloping forehead.

'Who's this, Jesse?' he said gutturally. There was no 'mister' here.

Johnson's look was just as suspicious. In the half-light his face had taken on once more that hungry wolfish look.

Apgood said: 'It's a man to see the boss, Monk.'

Monk said: 'Ur,' and stepped slowly, grudgingly aside.

The two men passed him. Johnson and he exchanged glances and in some subtle way, as brute beasts do, they seemed to understand each other.

Apgood turned a corner sharply. Johnson took it wide, he had all the mannerisms of the professional troubleshooter. It would take a smart man to 'jump' him – although the deceased Phil had almost done that.

This passage was a great contrast to the former one. It was wider and the walls were panelled in oak and had delicately-shaded lanterns at intervals. Soft carpet covered every inch of the floor and at the far end the lights gleamed on the walnut graining of a wide handsome door.

Apgood stopped at this door and rapped on it with his knuckles. One loud rap – three rapid softer ones.

The other side of the door something rumbled. It was like the growl of a bear awakened from his slumbers. Then a deep guttural voice said: 'Who is it?'

'Jesse.'

'Come in, Jesse.'

'I've got a friend with me.'

'What kind of a friend?'

'The young man I told you about.'

'All right. Bring your friend in, Jesse.'

Apgood opened the door slowly. The lush carpet on the floor continued on into the room. The gambler trod on it as if it were broken glass. At the end of the wide expanse was a huge desk. Behind this desk a huge man sat. A huge, fat, smiling man. His face and head were completely hairless.

The face was like a water-melon which had stood in the sun too long, the waxy pulp of it wrinkling and going a yellowish-brown. A mass of wrinkles with rolls of fat in between, blubbery lips and a little button of a nose; little button eyes, too, sunk in pouches of fat, black and shining like two little fat bugs.

The fat lips were stretched in a smile which revealed no teeth. The man's face, his double chin (he had no neck) were greasy with sweat. He wore no collar but his shirt was pink and silken. His gaudily-flowered vest was of silk too, and the fingers which lay still like white sausages on the desk were decorated by rings which flashed in the light from the huge crystal chandelier. Blazing light in the daytime, and needed too, for the panelled walls and exotically-decorated ceiling were bare of any windows or skylight.

Jesse Apgood said: 'This is Mr Mack Johnson, Boss . . . Mack, this is Mr Gruber. We call him "Boss".'

That was the name: that was the name Piercy had mentioned last night. Johnson's mind was racing as he moved nearer and took the huge paw that was extended to him. Boss Gruber did not get up, his hand was like a pad of rubber, but the grip was strong as it tightened.

'Glad to know you, Mack.'

Johnson did not say anything. There was that wolfish look about him again.

Gruber's toothless grin widened, his little black eyes almost disappeared in their pouches of blubber. His rings flashed as he waved his hands expansively and said: 'Sit down, gentlemen.'

His voice was guttural, yet had the slow, lilting caressing tone of the Deep South. His chair creaked as he settled back in it. He placed his fingers together

47

in front of him and regarded the two men and his little eyes disappeared altogether.

Johnson had another chance to weigh things up, to look around the room. It was large and sumptuous. All the chairs, like the one he sat in, were padded in red velvet.

Along two of the walls were glass-fronted shelves of books. Imposing books, in leather binding with gold lettering on their spines. There was a glass-fronted china cabinet, or showcase or something or other against another wall. This was packed with little china figurines and gold and silver ornaments and plate and all manner of precious things.

There was a long couch to match the chairs and, at the back of the fat man's desk, a huge black safe which looked strong enough to withstand a charge of blasting-powder.

Johnson's eyes came back to the strange imposing figure behind the desk. The fat man looked like he was going to sleep. His smile had faded; his lips were pursed, his double chins sunk into his neck. He looked on the point of snoring any moment.

Johnson looked at Apgood. The gambler was immobile. He was watching Boss but his smooth face revealed no expression whatsoever.

'What's the pitch?' said Johnson flatly.

'Boss's thinking,' said Apgood, in exactly the same tone of voice. The fat man's head shifted a little. The Deep Southern drawling voice rumbled, 'Mr Johnson is getting impatient. What do you know about him, Jesse?'

Apgood told all he knew, which was not much. But it seemed to satisfy Boss. He said: 'Would you like to work with me, Mr Johnson?'

'I didn't say I wanted work. This *hombre* said somep'n about a proposition.' He jerked a thumb at Apgood.

'It is a proposition. It pays more than any mere "work" could do. All my men are "propositioned". We haven't had any dissatisfaction in the ranks yet, have we, Jesse?'

'I don't want to join any ranks. I play a lone hand.'

'A man like you could do that, Mr Johnson. I may just give you hints from time to time and pay you well if you acted upon them.'

'You want me to carry a gun for you?'

'Would there be anything very terrible in that? You don't wear that gun for ornament – and Jesse tells me you're quick on the draw.'

'A man's gotta be quick on the draw in this country.'

'Yes, if he expects to use his gun a lot.'

This made an opening for another trend of conversation. Johnson did not take advantage of this opening. He said: 'So I carry a gun for you. So that ain't terrible, but it could be – for me. Who do I shoot and when?'

'You don't shoot anybody.'

'Would you mind putting your cards on the table, *amigo.*'

'My men don't as a rule call me *amigo.*'

'I'm not one of your men – yet. An' if you hire me I won't have joined the ranks – make no mistake about that.'

Boss turned his head slightly, looked at Apgood. 'Very ill-chosen that word 'ranks', Jesse.'

Apgood nodded. He said, 'I don't think Mack understands.'

49

Boss Gruber smiled again. 'I don't think Mack's dumb.'

'I didn't mean that—'

'I'm still here,' said Johnson harshly. 'An' I don't like folks talkin' across me as if I've already left.' He began to rise.

'Sit down, Mack,' said Boss.

As he spoke a train-whistle beeped. It sounded so close it might even have been in the room.

Boss held up one finger. His smile broadened. 'Hear that?'

He paused. Then he went on.

'El Paso is no longer the sleepy hollow it used to be. The railroad's growing, they have branches all over the place. Carriages are bringing folks in all the time. El Paso has a particular attraction for adventurers and sporting gentry who are finding things too hot for them elsewhere. This is new land, one of the golden places of the Golden West, young men are pouring in to make their fortune – suckers . . .' The voice was sharper at the end. Then it died away, rumbling deeply in the barrel-like chest.

'I'm not a gambler. I know nothing about suckers. How does all this concern me?'

'You're not a gambler in the accepted sense I know. But I am sure you have gambled in many other ways.'

'Everybody has to gamble sometimes,' said Mack Johnson.

Boss Gruber went off at a tangent. 'You heard that train-whistle. Another train packed with people. It might be packed with the people I am expecting, have been expecting for the last few days.'

'Has that got anythin' to do with me?'

'It might have.'

'Who *are* these people?'

Boss Gruber waved a hand, leaned back in his creaking chair. His eyes were sunken again. He said: 'Thugs and shoulder-hitters from "The Mudhole", gamblers from the Mississippi, girls from the East and the South – they all know Boss Gruber – they're all coming here to work for me.'

'In that case why hire me?'

'They don't know you – you don't know them. You're unbiased – and you're not the friendly type.'

'Thanks.'

'I speak truth.'

'So? Get on with it.'

'You could be in command of those people.'

'Why me?'

'You seem to have the necessary qualities for the job.'

'What's the matter with Jesse Apgood?'

'Jesse's got his own job to do. He presides over the gaming tables in my other establishment.'

That 'other establishment' was news to Mack Johnson. He said: 'How many establishments have you got?'

'Oh, quite a few – quite a few. And I hope to have more.' Gruber smiled expansively like a complacent, well-fed Cheshire Cat.

He went on, his voice rumbling. 'If you're on the run and whoever is after you happens to arrive in El Paso you'll have plenty of folks behind you.'

'I work for you – you cover me. You seem to take a lot for granted.'

'I'm a gambler. I never take anything for granted.
That's why I'm so successful.'

'You're purty sure of yourself.'

'Aren't you?'

Mack Johnson did not answer that. He rose slowly.

CHAPTER SIX

The Spinning Wheel was the name of Boss Gruber's 'other establishment'. *The Spinning Wheel* – the name had a soothing sound reminiscent of white-haired old ladies in homely cabins. But the illusion was dispelled by the look of the place, inside and outside. Particularly *inside*. Once inside it became evident right away from whence the establishment got its picturesque name.

There were mirrors all round the walls and along the back of the bar, except for one place: the dead centre.

This was taken up by a huge model of a roulette-wheel lifted up and suspended there as if pinned to the wall. It was a fixture all right and it did not spin although it was garish in red, black and gold and complete with a number of little white balls. It was a magnificent focal piece admired by all – except drunkards at the bar who often got the idea it was liable to fall on them.

One evening Mack Johnson sat beneath this wheel, sat on a high stool, the 'look-out' stool, from which he could watch the whole room and everybody who came through the huge swing-doors across the floor opposite him. He was so high up that he could not be seen from outside, even by anyone peering in at the windows. They had to come right inside before they could see the huge wheel and the colourfully dressed young man, with the hard face and the cold eyes, enthroned against it.

The people had come just as Boss Gruber had said they would – come to swell 'the ranks'. Thugs and shoulder-hitters, and river bullies and gunmen – and the women too. There was a troupe of them, under a hideous-looking Creole woman who called herself Madame Le Collette. They were beauties, many of them, though characterized by a crystally hardness. They knew all the tricks of all the 'games'; their main function was to separate the suckers from their money, and the powers-that-be were not particular how that was done – as long as it *was* done. If they could accomplish it by womanly wiles, so be it, but if they wanted the help of a few strong arms wielding blackjacks, knives, or the business ends of guns, they could have those too.

Already Boss Gruber had more folks working for him than anybody else in El Paso – even Luke Piercy. There were rumours that Luke was mighty sick about it. He knew which way the wind was blowing, he knew that if he did not play his cards just right, he would be squeezed out altogether, that Gruber wanted to be complete boss of El Paso. It had happened before in these Western towns – many of them virtually run by gamblers, under the very noses of law and order – such as it was. Steve Maginnis was a good lawman, he had a 'rep' that would frighten many. But he was just one, how many folks could he get behind him if it came to a showdown. He was just a man – and the Rio was deep and very muddy at the bottom.

Of late Mack Johnson had taken to sitting a lot on the high 'look-out' stool – ever since he himself had fired the previous holder of the job for being drunk while on duty. 'Fired' him in more senses than one, 'called him out'; and beaten him to the draw and killed him.

Strangely enough, Marshal Maginnis did nothing about this affair. It was as if he had not even heard of it. He was skating on thin ice: probably he did not even care how many of these hoodlums shot each other to ribbons as long as they did not embroil the steady townsfolk in their quarrels. But now there was a Gruber-Piercy feud, just bubbling yet, but liable to come to the boil any time. There were rumours that Piercy was waiting for a bunch of gunfighters to join him. Gunfighters from Abilene and Tombstone and Dodge City and one or two more notorious places where Piercy had 'stomped' before he settled in El Paso.

There was an air of uncomfortable tension over the border-town. It was getting too big for its breeches and was liable to burst wide open any moment. Boss Gruber began snapping up vacant lots as fast as he could get them and throwing up gimcrack buildings to catch the overflow from his two larger places. It was said he had tried to buy many of the shopkeepers out too and some were thinking of selling and lighting out for more peaceful quarters. Gruber put his girls in all over the place – in all the darkest holes and corners. El Paso was bursting with vice, every kind of vice under the sun.

Luke Piercy began buying up lots too. The race was on. As Mack Johnson sat in *The Spinning Wheel* that night he thought about that race, and his place in it. By all accounts, he was one of the 'favourites'.

Ever-alert, his gaze swept the room. The packed tables with the smooth-faced black-coated dealers, the round poker tables around the edge of the room, the roulette-wheels with their lady croupiers, the smart boy with his 'thimble-rig' outfit in the corner and the wide-eyed suckers around him trying to spot which thimble hid the pea, the small stage with the band playing upon it, the negro pianist who always got a big hand. A haze of tobacco smoke almost obscured the door, it was often a drawback. Johnson squinted, the better to see through it, watching the doors swing as people passed in and out.

Suddenly he stiffened, though anybody watching his immobile form and inscrutable face would not have been aware of that fact. A broad old man had come through the doors, was wending his way through the crowd towards the bar. Silver hair curled from beneath his battered slouch hat. His face was seamed, his eyes keen: they peered around the room as he walked. They looked up at the young man on the stool and passed on.

The old-timer bellied up to the bar. Johnson heard him call for rye. He took it and turned his back to the bar and watched the room as he sipped it. Mack Johnson slipped from his stool and walked along

56

behind the bar, looking too. He saw the people he sought. There were two of them and they were taking part in a poker game.

They rose as Johnson called them. One of the other players said hotly, 'Hey! You fellers can't walk off like that.'

'The boss wants us. We'll be back.'

'You ain't leavin' with all them chips.'

'Yeh?' The smaller of the two men turned.

'Hold it, Pecos,' said Johnson. He came through the trap in the bar.

The disgruntled player said, 'They're winning. 'They—'

'Dry up,' said Mack Johnson. 'They'll be back.'

The man subsided muttering. He did not want any trouble with that young hellion.

Pecos and his companion joined Johnson. 'We sure were cleaning them bozoes out, Mack,' said the small Texan gunfighter. He had a face as wrinkled as a walnut.

'You're durn' tootin'.' Bullocks, the other man, was given to platitudes. He looked his name: he was the strong-arm man of the team. These two, although they did not look the part, were a couple of the cleverest sharpers in Boss Gruber's employ.

Johnson gave them hurried instructions. They listened. The nut-brown face of Pecos was intelligent and inscrutable but Bullock's bovine visage held puzzlement. Pecos nodded swiftly. 'Come on, slob,' he said. Still looking a little bewildered, Bullock followed him.

Mack Johnson watched them go. He did not then

go back to his perch but moved through the crowd. He reached the door. A man lounged at either side of it. Both of them were armed; it was surprising how many people were armed in the place tonight, despite the marshal's no gun ordinance.

Johnson spoke to the man on the right hand side and watched him as he took his place on the look-out. Then Johnson went outside and along the boardwalk.

He turned in at the theatre. As he passed the pay-box the same woman leered at him whom he had seen on that stormy night not so long ago. But this time she said, 'Howdy, Mack.' He flipped his hand and went on into the theatre. There in the soft gloom he took a seat.

A troupe of girls in tights and spangles were kick-ing their legs about. The musical comedy known as *The Girls of Piute Buttes* was still going strong.

Another girl danced out in front of the others, struck a pose, and began to sing. She had a pleasant, husky voice and the lilt of a Southern accent. Her hair was honey-gold, her figure all that could be desired. When she finished her song and retired to the wings, the crowd went wild; stamping and clap-ping and whistling and shouting. She appeared again and took a bow. The crowd shouted for an 'encore' so she gave them another little song. As she did so Mack Johnson was slipping from his seat and walking along the side-aisle to the front of the theatre.

Miss Lucy Studamiere was the star of the show. Her name was now painted up outside the theatre: in letters quite as big as anything else out there, for El

58

Paso had taken her to its black heart. Probably because it did not see much of her except when she was on the stage – she was a reserved kind of girl: she was never seen in the nightspots and very seldom in the stores during the day time. She rode around the edges of the town on a paint-pony on sunny mornings but she did not take much notice of anyone, except for a nod, and perhaps a smile.

She finished her song, and bowed again, and took a curtain call, and another one. Then the curtain was finally down to stay and the show was over and the motley began to stream out into El Paso Street.

The 'girls' had a long low dressing-room behind the stage, but Miss Studamiere, being the star, had a little place to herself. With her mauve silk dressing gown flying from her shoulders, her white limbs flashing, she ran along the corridor, opened the door and went in. Then she stopped dead.

'Close the door,' said the man.

'Mack – you've never been here before. I thought you didn't want anybody to know. Where's Annie?' All this was spoken breathlessly in that husky lilting voice.

'I got rid of Annie. It ain't that I don't want anybody to know, Lucy – it's just that I don't want you to be mixed up in anything I do.'

'I wouldn't mind that, honey,' she said softly.

'You don't understand, *chiquita.*'

'I understand. A man has to be rough here to live.'

Something like a smile flitted across the man's lean face. 'Rough is hardly the word.'

He crooked his finger and she went across to him.

59

He caught hold of her around the shoulders and drew her close and kissed her. She clung to him for a moment then drew away.

'You were with that Louise Praline woman this morning,' she said.

'Oh, spying on me, uh?'

His voice was level, she could not tell whether he was angry or not.

'No, somebody just happened to mention it.'

'Who?'

The girl hesitated. Then she said: 'Jesse Apgood.'

He gripped her arms. She winced. He said softly, 'Have you been hobnobbing with that smooth-talking gink?'

'He's your friend, isn't he? Mack, you're hurting me!'

He let her go. 'He's my friend, yes. But I don't share my women with him,' he said brutally.

The girl's face flamed hotly. 'Oh, you beast. I just spoke to him that's all. You vile jealous beast. You have meals with that Praline woman and chat like old friends – maybe more – but I can't even look at another man. Get out of here. I—'

She gasped as, instead of going away, he started forward and grabbed hold of her again.

'Don't be silly, *chiquita*,' he said softly. 'Louise Praline just happened to sit at my table this morning, that's all.'

'I thought she was one of the other side—'

'What do you mean: the other side?'

'She works for Luke Piercy, doesn't she?'

'Yes, she does. If she didn't hate the sight of me

60

maybe I'd find a few things out, uh?'

'You brute!' flared the girl once more. 'You'd do anything. You—'

He held her roughly, stopped her mouth with a kiss. When he let her go she was trembling. She whispered, 'You sat at her table and tried to pump her about things, didn't you?'

'Yes. That's right. Nothing more. You're my girl. Hurry up and get dressed an' we'll go for a ride.'

The girl stood hesitantly for a moment, looking at him with wide violet eyes which shone brightly as if with unshed tears. Then she turned and went through a pair of curtains. They closed behind her. Mack Johnson sat on a stool before the dressing table and made himself a cigarette. His face was expressionless as he sat and smoked.

When Lucy Studamiere reappeared she was wearing a plain pink silk shirtwaist and a black skirt. The make-up, which remained on her face, gave her rather an incongruous look, like a little girl painted for a charade.

'I'd like to come there,' she said with a smile and Mack Johnson got up from his seat.

She took his place and he stood behind her and watched her take the grease-paint off her face with cream. There was something childish, almost doll-like about her; without her make-up she looked very unlike the dancing sprite of *The Girls of Piute Buttes*. In fact, she did not look any kind of a stage-girl at all. She should be home with mother, sitting on the porch overlooking the plantation, with her faithful negro Nanny beside her.

She said suddenly, 'Mack, please get away from the mirror – you make me nervous.'

'Do I?' he said. He did not move right away and he saw her shiver.

'What's biting you?' he said, and moved then.

'Nothing, nothing at all. Where are we going, Mack?'

'Just a ride I guess. Down by the Rio maybe.'

'You like that river, don't you, Mack?' she said softly.

He did not answer immediately and she turned her head and looked at him. For the first time since she had known him, since she had been introduced to him by Gruber, the man who was putting on her show, she saw a little puzzled frown creasing his brow.

When he finally spoke it was almost as if he was talking to himself.

'Yes I like the Rio. I've never seen another river like it. It's like a living thing. Sometimes when I'm down there I feel like I want to talk to it, tell it things. It could tell me a lot more than I could ever tell, I guess. It's seen some things has that river. It seems to be slower an' more thoughtful than any other river.'

He saw the girl looking at him and he stopped talking. His tan went a little darker. He said: 'I'm babbling like a crazy man.'

'You're not. I think the Rio's like a living thing myself sometimes. But I don't like it. The waters are bad, evil – it's all bad!'

CHAPTER SEVEN

'There's good an' bad in everything, *chiquita*,' said Mack Johnson.

Five minutes later they left the theatre by the back door. They saw nobody. They went along the backs of El Paso Street until they came to Jarrold's Hotel. Although actually run by Sim Jarrold, and bearing his name, this place belonged to Boss Gruber. It was the swellest place in town and most of the 'top boys' (including Mack) and many of the girls, too, had apartments there. Lucy and her troupe had rooms there.

The man and the girl did not go inside the hotel but entered the large stables behind it. Here Lucy saddled up her paint – while Mack began to do the same with a black horse.

The girl turned. 'That's not yours, is it, Mack. Where's your pony?'

'I lent him to someone,' he said. 'So I'm borrowing this one.'

'Oh, who does he belong to?'

'I ain't sure.'

'Oh,' she said again, and left it at that.

They led the horses out of the stables and mounted them. They rode out of town. Mack turned towards the river. Lucy followed him without comment. Neither of them spoke for a while. It was the girl who finally broke the silence. 'I've only got another fortnight here, Mack.'

'Have you? Where do you go after that?'

'We've got a date in Rincon.'

'New Mexico, uh?'

'Yes.'

'You'll have to cross the ol' river then?'

She was uncertain what he actually meant by that remark. She said: 'There are bridges, aren't there?'

'Yeh – so they tell me.'

He stopped talking then, riding silently, upright, as if he was part of the horse. The arrogant power of him seemed to flow out and encompass the girl, so that she feared she would never escape from it. Rincon was such a long way away: she dreaded leaving El Paso, wild as it was, and going there. Was it because of Mack that she felt this way? What was this power he had over her? People said he was bad. If he was really bad would she feel for him as she did? Was it love she felt for him, or was it some strange form of fear, fascination?

Who was Mack Johnson? Where did he come from? What was he before he came to El Paso and became Boss Gruber's right-hand man? What was the power about him, apart from his fighting ability, intelligence and quickness on the draw, which had gotten him to this position in so short a time? He was not even scared of that horrible Gruber himself like all the rest of them were.

The girl's thoughts were broken into by his voice, that deep uncompromising voice which held in it no cajolery, that she thought could never hold any pity.

'How long you gonna carry on with this game, Lucy? It isn't the game for a girl like you.'

'You mean the stage?'

'Yeh.'

'It's my life, Mack. Ever since I was a little girl I've wanted to be an actress. Many people – even in my home town – think it's a cheap and common profession. But it isn't.'

'I didn't say it was. But moseying around the countryside isn't the life for a girl like you.'

'I'm no better and no worse than most girls.'

'Aren't you? How about your parents – what do they think about it?'

'I haven't any parents, Mack. They both died six years ago. I've only an uncle and aunt who were my guardians. I don't think they bother much what happens to me.'

'I didn't know about your parents. I'm sorry.'

The girl looked at him. It seemed a little out of character for Mack Johnson to be sympathetic. Although he was more gentle with her than he was with anybody else – or at least she thought so. Probably he was as gentle with her as it was possible for a man of his calibre to be. Did that mean he cared for her? He acted as if he did. Her mind was on the hurdy-gurdy once more. She spoke quickly to alleviate her thoughts.

'Nobody molests a troupe of girls travelling the

country – even in the Wild West. We're getting quite famous. We give entertainment – often in places where the only other entertainment is drink and gambling. We are a welcome change – and men look up to us. Why – if any man was to molest me, or any member of my troupe, he would be lynched by his friends.'

'Yeh. I guess you're right. But I still think—'

She interrupted him, speaking quickly again, the words bursting from her before she could stop them. 'Can you offer anything better?'

He did not answer her right away. Her heart was in her throat.

Finally he said: 'No, *chiquita*, I can't offer anything better.' Then, so softly that she hardly heard him: '*I wish I could.*'

They were silent then, riding side by side, close together. A new feeling came over the girl. She was surprised at it, for it was almost like pity.

The plain of short grass, interspersed by groves of trees and outcrops of boulders, was washed by moonlight. The ground began to slope as they approached the Rio Grande and finally they saw it below them. It was a ribbon of silver, twisted and crumpled and thrown down there carelessly by a giant hand. There were dark shades here and there along its edges as if something waited, brooding there. That was a queer fancy which entered Lucy's mind as her eyes were fixed on the river and she rode slowly down toward it. She disliked it, saying it was bad, and yet there was something about it which fascinated her. Mack had said there was good and bad in everything. Did he hold the same dark fascination for her that the river did? There was something about him that was so very like the river. Something dark and brooding, yet wild and untamed. They were friends, the river and he.

Lucy shook these queer fancies from her head as he spoke to her. But it was almost as if he echoed her thoughts.

'There it is – the Rio. I owe quite a lot to that river, it's been a friend to me.'

She waited for him to go on but he did not. Suddenly she realized she was afraid to ask the question which trembled on her lips. She left it unspoken.

They rode down to the bank of the river and dismounted from their horses. They stood looking across the water, shimmering in the moonlight, sucking, beckoning, but with very little current.

The man said: 'Let's walk along a piece,' and they turned their horses' heads and led them along the bank. Suddenly he said, 'Listen!'

Faintly in the distance came the sound of drumming hoofs.

'Quite a bunch by the sound of it,' said Johnson. 'Comin' from the direction of Cripple Creek.'

'Yes,' said the girl.

Even as their voices died away the distant sound was dying with them, becoming part of the soughing night wind, dying away altogether.

The couple, with their horses, continued along the bank of the river towards a small grove of trees, the edge of which angled out across the water. They were gaunt trees, little shelter at all. But cover from the pale moonlight reflected in the river. The girl seemed to hasten her pace as they got nearer.

The man was looking about him. He said: 'Those horses aren't comin' back this way, are they?'

'I can't hear anything.'

'I thought I did – imagination I guess.'

Along here the banks were rocky. They were ranged by outcrops of rocks. They were passing a large pile, fantastic in the moonlight, and were almost at the edge of the grove of trees when Johnson whirled suddenly. He pushed the girl, shouting 'Down', his other hand drawing his gun.

Lucy's horse squealed in agony and the night was hideous with gunfire. The girl flung herself for the shelter of the trees. Something whined over her head. Something thunked into the trunk of a tree as she reached it. She hit the ground and rolled. When she stopped she was in shelter, lying on her stomach, looking out.

Johnson's horse, snorting with terror, whipped past her. Lucy's horse lay motionless on its side and Johnson lay flat behind it, his hat off, his head uplifted a little.

She saw his face in the moonlight and she shuddered. There were new lines on it, his mouth was stretched in a snarl. He looked different, like an animal waiting to pounce, a hungry wolf. She knew then the meaning of his power, why people were scared of him. He was not a man now, he was a fighting machine, utterly merciless.

The breeze sighed and there was no more sound

as they waited. A thudding in her ears almost deaf-
ened the girl. She was startled until she realized it
was her heart beating. The outcrop of rock from
which flame and lead had spurted a few seconds
before was silent, white in the moonlight, one edge
of it rippling with the shadows from the trees.

It was this corner on which Johnson's eyes seemed
to be fixed. He was motionless. He looked as if he
could stay like that for ever, raised a little on one
elbow, his gun level in his hand, his head uplifted but
hidden by the flank of the dead horse.

His hat was on the ground a little way behind him.
The girl watched his free hand reach back, almost as
if it had no relation whatever to his body, and grasp
the brim and draw the hat towards him. He moved it
mechanically and his eyes were on the corner of the
rocks all the time. His face had a set carven look. He
raised the hat, then with a flick of his wrist thrust it
above the horse's rump.

The shadows on the rock widened and, even as
flame blossomed and gunfire thundered, he was
rising; half-crouching, leaping for the trees. He
reached a trunk just in front of Lucy and was upright
behind it, fanning the hammer of his gun.

A man rose from behind the rocks and was stiffened against the sky. Lucy saw his contorted face, his
glaring eyes, his wide-open mouth. She knew he was
screaming but she heard no sound above the
hideous din of the gunfire.

There was a gun in the man's hand; it dangled, he
tried to bring it level. His body shuddered as more
bullets thudded into it. Then he crumpled suddenly

and became part of the shadows once more: still, silent.

The gun-smoke drifted and Lucy tried hard not to cough as it stung her throat and nostrils. It made her eyes smart too, for they were wide open and staring.

Johnson half-turned his head. 'Stay down,' he said. 'There's another one – maybe more.'

He was taking shells from his belt and swiftly reloading his gun. She nodded wordlessly but did not know whether he had seen her or not. He was turned sideways so that his body was completely hidden behind the tree. His gun was held ready, uplifted a little. His face was barred by shadows, which gave it a broody, saturnine look. He did not seem aware of the girl any more.

She lay and watched him and watched the edge of the rocks beyond him. She listened. The wind sighed and, behind her, the river made a sound like an old man mumbling to himself. A rather wicked old man, she thought. She felt like giggling at this sudden irrational fancy. There was a quality of unreality about everything. Like a dream she had dreamed. She had dreamed about coming to the Wild West, the romantic West of the pioneers. Her dream had come true and she had found the reality to be nothing but a lot of dirt and heat and noise.

But this was the real thing. This *was* the Wild West, and that man before her – her friend, her lover – he was a gunfighter. And behind those rocks lay a dead man and another man, maybe more, living: 'bushwackers', waiting to kill or be killed. Playing cat and mouse.

But which was the cat – and which was the mouse?

CHAPTER EIGHT

The wind sighed mournfully and the river mumbled on telling its own tales of action and bloodshed. And here was another tale to add to its repertoire – as the men waited, and the woman too, and the blue powder-smoke drifted away in the moonlight. Behind the rocks there was a faint rattling sound. Further away a horse whinnied softly.

The girl almost rose in screaming tension as Johnson moved suddenly from behind the tree, threw himself forward, his gun blazing. His wolfish face was lit intermittently by the flashes for a second then she could see it no more. He fell on his stomach and she crammed her fist into her mouth to stifle a cry. He had been hit! No, he hadn't! He was up again, diving for the cover of a tree on the very edge of the clearing. Shots ripped the night to shreds and the flashes defied the moonlight; then he was in safety and she saw his upper body heaving as he dragged air.

She thought she could guess what he was making for: a smaller bunch of rocks a little divided from the main outcrop. If he could reach those he would be almost flanking the other man. It seemed to her now that there was only one of them.

A cry rose to her lips, but she stifled it fearfully, as Johnson moved again. He moved from behind the tree, incredibly swiftly, on all fours almost, as he ran for the rocks. Nothing happened and she realized the other man must be retreating.

Johnson reached his objective, skirted them swiftly, and vanished behind them. Again the heavens seemed to split apart and gunfire rattled and echoed away over the river. She could not wait any longer and without a thought for her own safety rose and began to run towards the smaller rocks.

As she reached them she threw herself forward and rolled. Explosions were in her ears. She hit her head on something and for a moment things were hazy around her.

She rose to her knees and then she saw Johnson. He was crouching, poking out. Obviously he had not heard her approach. As she watched he rose. Then he flung himself sideways, his body twisting. As he came upright again his gun was flaming.

Lucy saw the other man. Only for a moment and then he was gone. Then the night was silent and the smoke was drifting back to her and Johnson was drawing himself upright. She saw him level his gun. Then he fired – once only – and she knew he was making sure. She felt no horror. He had fought for his life – and probably hers too. If the others had lost the only thing she could do was be grateful that was how it had been.

Johnson climbed over the small boulders and

walked forward. He stopped and Lucy rose and followed him. He whirled, his eyes blazing, his mouth stretched.

'*Mack*!'

He stiffened, yet the gun in his hand seemed to tremble. 'What a damn' fool thing to do,' he said huskily. 'I nearly shot you.'

She stood staring at him, her lips forming little inarticulate phrases. All she managed to get out was: 'I'm sorry!'

When he spoke again his voice was softer. 'Go back to the horses, Lucy. I'll follow you.'

As she moved away she realized he had spoken almost unconsciously, mainly to reassure her. There were no horses. One of them was dead, the other had bolted. With the bit between his teeth he was probably heading for home. She went back to the carcase of the other horse, the little paint. Since hiring him in El Paso she had gotten attached to the pony. She had thought of buying him outright and taking him with her somehow when the troupe moved. She turned away from the body and looked out across the river. Standing like that she could imagine nothing had happened.

She heard footsteps, and the sound of iron-shod hoofs ringing on rock. She turned. Mack was approaching, leading two horses. He left them and came across to her. She half-turned away from him and he caught hold of her shoulders. She shrank from him a little but he gripped her tightly.

'Take it easy, *chiquita*,' he said.

She began to tremble, her whole body began to

tremble. She shrank no more but turned to him, clung to him. He held her tightly and did not say anything and gradually the trembling subsided.

'I'm all right now,' she said and tried to draw away.

He let her go and turned towards the dead horse.

'Pity,' he said. 'He was a nice little beast.'

He bent and stripped the carcase of the saddle and other accoutrements. These he piled on the front of one of the other beasts.

'Come on, Lucy,' he said.

As she got into the saddle and looked at him there was a question in her eyes.

He said: 'Two Piercy men.'

'Mack – are you going to leave them there?'

'What else can I do? They'll be picked up later.' He mounted the horse with the extra stuff on its back and urged it forward. She followed.

As they approached the lights of El Paso he said, 'Would you mind walking the rest of the way, Lucy?'

'No – o . . . Why?'

'I want to send these horses home.'

They both dismounted and he took the spare gear from the one horse. He slapped them both on their flanks with his free hand. As they cantered away he said: 'No message is needed. I guess Piercy 'ull know what's happened.'

'Mack – do you think Piercy sent them?'

'He sent them all right. Not particularly for tonight maybe, but just with orders to get me when they had the chance. Them two bozoes saw their chance – it didn't worry them that there was a woman along too.'

'You can't prove Piercy sent them, Mack.'

'I don't need any proof – I know.'

'Mack – you're not going to—' She was increasingly inarticulate.

'Not quite yet. Don't worry, *chiquita.*'

With that she had to be content, for he obviously did not want to talk about it any more. They approached the town from the back, taking the same unmarked trail they had used when they came out. He kissed her. She clung to him, trying to find words. They would not come. He pushed her gently away.

'Go in now,' he said. 'Don't tell anybody about this.'

'All right.' She backed away from him.

'Be careful, Mack,' she whispered, and ran to the back door of the hotel. He watched her until the door closed behind her.

He turned away with a gesture that was almost savage, and kicked a tin can which was in his path. Then he froze, looking around him as the clatter died away. To him came the harsh buzz of the town. But there was no other sound out here. He walked on a little further then through an alley into El Paso Street. A few yards along the boardwalk and he reached the theatre. He did not pass anybody on the way. He used his own key to open the little door. He closed it behind him and went on along the bare, dimly-lit corridor. Monk came forward to meet him.

'The marshal's been lookin' for you,' he said. 'I dunno what he wanted.'

'Yeh. I gotta see him. Boss in?'

'Yeh.' Monk moved aside. Johnson went past him

arrogantly and turned into the wider carpeted corridor.

The door at the end opened and Jesse Apgood came through. The two men approached each other, then stopped.

'Mack, the marshal's been looking for you.'

'I know. I heard.'

'Oh, Monk told you I guess.' Apgood made as if to pass. Johnson barred his way. He said: 'We're pards, Jesse – remember? Keep away from Lucy Studamiere. Stop telling her things about me.'

'Mack. I only—'

'Just don't tell her things about me.'

Apgood made to pass again. This time Johnson let him. The gambler said: 'I don't have to take orders from you.'

'All right, Jesse,' said Johnson.

Apgood turned swiftly. For a moment there was fear in his eyes. Johnson's back was moving away from him.

A look of hate came into the gambler's eyes. His hand dropped to his belt.

He was still standing there with his hand at his belt when the door closed behind Johnson. He had not even knocked. Nobody else could walk in on Boss Gruber that way. When, a few minutes later, Johnson left the office, Apgood had gone. But Monk still slouched around in the passage. He said eagerly: 'I forgot to tell yuh, Monk, a bunch of tough-lookin' *hombres* rode into town about half-an-hour ago. We thought they was them gunnies Piercy's been goin' to get – but they went straight to the marshal's office.'

'Yeh, I know. Boss told me about it.'

'Uh – I guess Apgood told Boss.'

As he went out into the street Johnson figured that the bunch of riders must be the horsemen Lucy and he had heard as they were moving along the river, before the bushwackers opened up. They had seemed to be coming from the direction of Cripple Creek. He wondered who they were.

He went straight on to the marshal's office and knocked at the door. A voice said, 'Come in,' and he entered. Steve Maginnis sat behind his desk. Charlie was lounging on a bench against the wall. There did not seem to be anybody else present.

'I hear you've been looking for me, Marshal.'

'Yes, sit down, Mack.'

Johnson drew out the chair from the other side of the desk, swivelled it round and straddled it, his arms across the back.

The marshal shoved a packet of cigarettes across the desk. Johnson took one. The marshal took one himself and tossed one to Charlie. The deputy caught it deftly: he was no longer lounging.

The three men lit up. Steve Maginnis blew smoke-rings. Then he said: 'I had an old gent call on me tonight. He owns a little spread the other side o' the river – in New Mexico. He told me a story. It seems he was out riding a few weeks ago when he was held up by a young feller on foot. One of his horses was shot and he was pitched out and knocked unconscious. Some of his boys found him lying in his own wagon, where this thoughtful hold-up man must have put him. He had severe concussion. He might've died.'

77

'What's all this got to do with me?'

'I dunno, Mack. Just let me tell you the story though. Just to please me, uh?'

'All right. Go ahead.'

'Seemed like all the hold-up man stole was a horse. The other two horses, which had bolted – there were four horses in the team you see – the other two horses arrived back home. The old man's fond of his horses and this one was the pick of the bunch. As soon as he was fit enough he came out to look for it – and to look for the skunk who stole it, and almost killed him to boot. He'd only caught a glimpse of the bandit and knew he was lean and young. He had been dirty, ragged, in need of a shave – the old man wasn't sure whether he'd recognize him if he saw him again. But he knew he'd recognize the horse if he saw it again. He could also prove that it belonged to him. All his horses wore his brand on their flanks – a cross and a six – and the stolen one was no exception.'

Maginnis took one last deep drag at his cigarette and flipped the stub away. Then he went on: 'After a while he figured the bandit may have forded the river – he'd hardly get down into the pass from where he was. Finally the old man finished up in El Paso, the nearest town to the river if the bandit was crazy enough to swim it. He came to me and told me his story – dates an' all. What seemed a great coincidence to me was that the day he was held up was the very same day that you arrived in the town. The night you arrived I should say.'

'What are you getting at?'

'I'm a lawman, Mack, I'm allus *getting* at somep'n or other. D'yuh remember that night, Mack? It was pouring with rain, you an' your horse were half-drowned. D'yuh remember how I asked you about your horse – a mare it was – she looked like she came through the river. You had no saddle on her either. You said you came from Cripple Creek – you said you'd lost your saddle in a crapgame there. Charlie went an' seen the marshal of Cripple Creek – that's Bill Ransome, he's a friend o' mine. They got to talking and Bill said he didn't know of any tough looking young stranger who'd been in the town that day – or the day before, or any other day round about that time. An' he was quite sure nobody had lost a saddle in a crapgame.'

'That's right,' said Charlie.

'What are you aiming at?' said Johnson. 'Why are you so eager to trip me up?'

'You're an interesting character, Mack. I'd like to know everything about you. I think it might be an interesting story. Furthermore, I think a man would have to be mighty smart to succeed in tripping you up.'

'Quit the smart talk an' come to the point.'

'All right, Mack. Wal, after Charlie came back from Cripple Creek I got to thinking – an' when this old-timer turned up with his tale of a mysterious bandit I got to thinkin' a heap more. Me an' Charlie went to Pueblo's an' asked to see your horse. Pueblo was in a panic. He said your horse had been stolen while he was down the street having a drink and what you'd do to him when you found out he could not imagine.'

'Why, the fat skunk – what does he mean? Where is the horse?'

'Nobody knows, Mack – except the people who stole it. It seemed a mighty big coincidence to me that the horse happened to vanish just as I wanted to have a look at it. I asked Pueblo if he remembered seeing a brand on the horse's flank. He said maybe, he wasn't sure. A smart Mexican, Pueblo, he always takes the middle course.'

'I'll skin him – letting my hoss go like that!'

'So you didn't know the horse had been stolen?'

'No, it's news to me. I can see what you're getting at though, and I don't like it.'

'Am I getting at something?'

'You talk too much,' said Johnson curtly. 'You wrap your meanings up in cottonwool. You think I'm the bandit who held up the old man – and the vanished horse is the one who belonged to him. But you've got nothing to go on so you're acting cagey.'

Charlie rose. Johnson watched him out of the corner of his eye. With the other one he watched the marshal.

The latter said: 'Sit down, Charlie. Mr Johnson doesn't mean to be insulting. And, in a way, he's quite right in what he says.'

He looked directly at Johnson again and although there was a little smile beneath the black bar of his moustache his eyes were like steel.

CHAPTER NINE

'Yes, Mack, I'm pretty certain that you are the one who held up the old man and took his horse. But, like you say, I have nothin' to go on. Furthermore, even if I had something to go on I could not do much about it. The old man comes from New Mexico, the crime was committed in New Mexico – out of my jurisdiction altogether, but the oldtimer's a vengeful old goat – I guess anybody would be in his case – he's liable to overlook things like that. If he sees the man he's after he's liable to take the law into his own hands.'

'So you're warning me. That's very kind of you, marshal.' Johnson's unemotional voice was as mocking as it could be.

'In a way I am warning you. I shouldn't like anything to happen to you – not here anyway – the town might blow up. You're such a damned important person, Mack. I almost think sometimes that you oughta be wearing my badge. I shouldn't like anything to happen to the old man either, Mack. Do you understand?'

'I think I get your drift, marshal. I don't make war on old men.'

'Don't you?' said the marshal.

Johnson leaned forward. Charlie started. Johnson turned his head and looked at him. 'What's the matter, *amigo*?'

Charlie scowled and said nothing. Johnson looked again at the marshal and said: 'I must thank you for telling me the news about my horse being stolen. I'll send out a search-party right away. Now I have some news for you.'

Maginnis matched his mockery with another smile. 'Shoot,' he said.

'I went down by the river tonight. Two of Piercy's men tried to bushwack me. I killed them both.' Maginnis sat upright in his seat. Charlie rose, came across to the desk and glowered down at Johnson. Maginnis said: 'This straight?'

'It's straight all right.'

'They bushwacked you – but you killed them? An' you ain't even scratched?'

'That's right. I just happened to shoot faster an' straighter that's all.'

'Are you sure some of your boys didn't do the bushwacking?'

Johnson rose, kicking his chair back. 'I've stood enough. I don't have to stand any more.'

Charlie backed away from the desk, his hand at his belt. 'Go on,' said Johnson softly. 'There's two of yuh.'

The marshal sat still. 'Don't be a fool, Mack,' he said. 'Sit down. Have another smoke.'

Johnson stiffened as the lawman's hand moved. But Maginnis merely pushed the packet of cigarettes across the desk once more. 'Relax, Charlie,' he said out of the corner of his mouth.

Johnson sat down and took a cigarette. 'You're a cool customer, Mr Marshal,' he said.

'I could say the same about you.' Maginnis tossed a cigarette to Charlie who, scowling horribly, had gone back to his perch against the wall. The three men lit up. The marshal said: 'Whereabouts did this happen?'

'Level with the town. The two men must've watched me leave an' got in ahead o' me. They were behind some rocks. One of them moved too quickly and I spotted him. I took cover in some trees.'

'An' you got them both?'

'Yeh, in the front too.'

'I have no doubt of that, Mack,' said Maginnis suavely. 'Er – did you walk to the river?'

'No, I rode.'

'Not on the mare surely?'

'No, I was just going for a canter so I borrowed one from the stables in back o' the hotel. The hoss belonged to one of my men.'

'You were alone? Nobody else with you?'

'I said I was alone, didn't I?'

'All right, Mack. That's all you need tell me. I don't think you'll be leaving town yet. I'll send Charlie for you if I want you.'

'How about picking up Piercy? They were his men, the back-shooting skunks.'

'You know better than that, Mack. You know I couldn't hold him.'

'No. I guess not,' said Johnson softly. He rose and made for the door.

The marshal called him and he turned. Maginnis said: 'Did you know there was a troop of Texas Rangers in town, Mack?'

'So that was who the tough-looking riders were everybody's bin talkin' about. What are they doing here?'

'Oh, just passing through. But they might stay a while.'

'Did you send for 'em?'

'Nope. But I can always get a troop if I want one. I useter be a Ranger myself.'

'Yeh, so I've heard – made quite a name for yourself, didn't you?'

'Fine service the Rangers.'

'I wouldn't know.'

'It's a matter of opinion, I guess. I just thought I'd tell you they were here, Mack, in case you thought of blowing up Luke Piercy's *Golden Hall* tonight. You wouldn't want to get the town a bad name an' have a troop of Rangers billeted here for good, would you, Mack?'

'You told me,' said Johnson.

The door closed behind him. Charlie's scowl faded. He began to grin.

Mack Johnson was cursing himself as he went along the boardwalk. There was something he had forgotten. He was moving fast when he went through the swing-doors of *The Spinning Wheel*. Nothing so common as hard-wearing bat-wings for Boss Gruber's garish establishment. He had proper swing-doors, frosted-glass tops with cherubs painted all over them.

Mack elbowed his way to the bar. He acknowledged greetings with jerks of his head. He bellied up to the bar and shouted for a large rye. As the barman bustled to get it Johnson turned away from the bar. Pecos and Bullock had resumed their game of poker.

Pecos caught Johnson's eye and, disregarding the protest of the other players, rose and came across to him.

'We did that job all right, Mack,' he said softly. 'She's hidden in the old mine workings. Nobody'll find her there.'

'All right. Now I've got another job for yuh. Another horse job.'

'Aw, Mack, the game was going swell—'

'This is an easier way of making yourself some bonus.'

'All right.'

'Take the trail to the Rio right outside town. When you get to the banks move along to the right for about two hundred yards. There's an' outcrop of rocks one side – and a grove of trees on the water's edge.'

'I know the place.'

'There's a dead horse there. It's been shot. I want you to roll it into the river. Make sure there's no sign left of it.'

Pecos's small brown face showed no puzzlement. Until Johnson's next words.

'There are a couple of dead men hehind the rocks. Piercy men who I had a run in with. Don't go near 'em, try not to leave any footprints. You'll have to work fast because the marshal knows about this an' he'll be going out to pick up them bodies. Make a detour on your way back. Now tell Bullock an' get going, pronto.'

'Sure, Mack.' Pecos turned away. Johnson caught his arm. 'If either of you breathe a word about this – the dead horse I mean – I'll have you skinned alive.'

Pecos looked aggrieved. 'Gosh, Mack, you know us.'

He went to Bullock and told him to come along. One of the other players began to expostulate hotly.

'Shut up,' snarled Pecos. Bullock growled something too as he raked in his winnings. The man shut up. Johnson watched the two men until they left the place. Then he turned and grabbed his rye and tossed it off as if he was a very thirsty man. He called for another.

He took that and holding it in his hand turned with his back to the bar and surveyed the room. The look-out on the high stool caught his eye and gave a languid wave of his hand to convey that all was well.

As far as Johnson was concerned all was well too. He turned back to the bar, downed his drink and called for another. He was looking at pictures in his glass when out of the corner of his eye he saw the look-out give a faint movement, like a signal. He turned his head. The lookout raised his eyebrows and inclined his head towards the door. Johnson swivelled his head a little further. He peered through the smoke-haze and finally saw the marshal worming his way through the mob. He turned back to his glass and from under lowered lids watched the lawman's approach.

Maginnis was alone. He was dawdling and looking around him. Finally he spotted Johnson at the bar and came over to him. The young man did not turn until the lawman touched his elbow.

'Hallo, Steve,' he said.

'Hallo, Mack.' The marshal hailed the barman and asked for a short beer.

The man raised his eyebrows insolently. 'We don't get much call for that kind of stuff, marshal.'

'Get it,' said Mack Johnson curtly.

'Sure, Mack.' The man bustled away.

Maginnis said: 'They sure jump to it when you talk to 'em, don't they?'

'Yeh – I guess they do,' said Johnson.

People at the bar had moved away from the two men: the Gruber *segunda* and the slow-talking trouble-shooter with the black moustache. Maybe they expected something to start.

Johnson echoed their thoughts when he said, 'You don't often honour us with your presence, marshal.'

'Wal, to tell you the truth, Mack, I was looking for that old-timer I told you about. I wouldn't want him to get lost in a strange town.'

'Have you seen him?'

'Nope. Maybe he's left.'

'I ain't seen any strange old man in here. What's he look like?'

Maginnis smiled. 'Do you really want to know, Mack?'

'Hell – whadyuh think I asked you for?'

'Well, he's a well-built old buzzard. Broad, upright. Must've been quite a good-looker in his day. Square, lined face. Blue eyes – pretty keen. A good mop of hair for his age: long, curling down his neck. Silver.'

'Wait a minute,' said Johnson. He turned, crooked a finger to the look-out. The fellow got down from his stool and came across. Johnson repeated the sheriff's description to him.

'Have you seen an old-timer like that in here? A stranger?'

The man pondered for a bit then said, 'Yeh, I saw an old man like that once tonight. Now I come to think about it I noticed him particularly. He seemed to be looking for something.'

'How long was this ago?' said the marshal.

'Oh, an hour, mebbe more. Didn't you see him, Mack? I think you were here.'

Maginnis looked keenly at Johnson, who said: 'If I was in here I don't remember seeing him. Has he been in since?'

'He ain't been in while I've been up on that stool. He wasn't here but a few minutes the first time.

'All right, Arnie. Thanks. Get back on the job.'

'Sure, Mack.'

The marshal said: 'It must be quite a job bein' Boss Gruber's right-hand man.'

'Yeh,' said Johnson noncommittally.

Maginnis went on, 'Even so I still can't understand why you joined up with Boss Gruber in the first place.'

'Why?'

'Well, I figured you for a lone wolf. The sort who wouldn't take orders from anybody.'

'I don't take orders.'

'You must do. You're Boss's *segunda*. He pays yuh don't he?'

'Yeh, sure, he pays me. But he leaves the running o' most things to me.'

'But he's the power – he's the brains.'

Johnson shrugged. 'All right, have it your own way.'

'I ain't trying to rile you, Mack. I'm just thinking aloud.'

The marshal started to talk again. He still sounded like he was thinking aloud.

'He's no good to you, Mack. Just the same as he's no good to anybody here. He thinks money can buy anything – and the damnable thing is he's got a good many other people believing it, too. He's not our kind. He's a graduate from the gambling boats of the Mississippi and Red River. A tinhorn gambler that's all he was before he got too fat and idle, before the law started clearing the rivers and sweeping the rats away. Then, like a good many of his kind, he came West – far West where there ain't so much law. But the law is catching up, Mack. Him an' all his kind 'ull soon be finished for ever.'

The marshal paused. Johnson said: 'I didn't know you were such a purty speechifier, Steve.'

The marshal smiled. 'Didn't you? I'm an old mossyhorn, Mack. I've got some old-fashioned ideas an' sometimes I get kind of carried away by them. I hate people like Boss Gruber who pay other people to do their gunning an' dirty work for them. He's scum, Mack, river scum, he's no good to you or anybody else. If things went wrong for him, and you

89

were in the way, he'd have you stabbed in the back and thrown in the river quicker'n batting an eyelash. His sort have no loyalty, no pity, no friends. A killer like the Apache Kid is a saint compared to a filthy skunk like Boss Gruber.'

The marshal stopped talking. He was smiling again. Johnson said: 'What are you trying to do, Steve, frighten me with the bogey man? I can take care of myself.'

'That's what I thought you'd say.' Maginnis downed his drink and turned away from the bar.

'Anybody gone to fetch those bodies in?' said Johnson softly.

'Yes, Charlie and Pete. They should be back pretty soon. See you, Mack.'

'See you.' Johnson watched the marshal's tall form until it disappeared through the swing-doors.

He turned to the bar once more and crooked his finger to the barman. When the man came across with the bottle he took it from him.

'All right, Joe. I'll pour it myself.'

'Sure, Mack.'

Sure, Mack. The phrase echoed in his brain. It was like a hurdy-gurdy refrain.

He figured that maybe he had had too much to drink. But as a rule he could stand much more. So he poured himself another one.

CHAPTER TEN

It was half-an-hour later, maybe more, when he began to move. The place was in full swing; a blue haze of smoke hung like a diaphanous curtain beneath the lamps. All was noise: the music, the voices, the singing, the laughter, the bankers intoning the odds. But, as Mack Johnson moved, to him there was nothing. People stepped aside to let him through and as he passed them it was as if they were not there. His eyes were fixed on the door; like an automaton he made for it; he was alone with his purpose.

Maybe the drink had brought on the final decision, had turned the pride into hate and then crystallized the hate. Maybe the marshal had riled him after all. But the drink was nothing, the noise was nothing, the people were nothing. Him, and his purpose: they were the only real things.

Men saw his eyes and his face, his expression set and wolfish. A man who had not seen his face said 'So-long, Mack' cheerily as he passed through the doors into the night.

He turned left sharply. His boot-heels went clack-

clack on the boardwalk. His back was straight and his arms dangled at his side but did not swing.

A man passed him and said, 'Howdy, Mack' but he did not answer. The man stared after him curiously, went on, turned to stare again, then stood outside *The Spinning Wheel* and watched him go into another brilliantly-lit place further along the street. After that the man went quickly through the doors of *The Spinning Wheel*. He looked a little startled.

Mack Johnson slowed down, blinking beneath the strong lights of the other hall: *The Golden Hall*, the enemies' stronghold. Awareness of what he was up against returned to him slowly but it did not weaken his resolve. He was icy-cold. He looked at the faces around him. The staring faces. None of them had any features. He felt like spitting at them.

He heard the sounds: the voices, the music, and all the rest of it. He heard it now, heard it die a little as the faces turned to stare at him. Then he was going through the crowd and the people were moving aside to let him pass like they always did.

From up on the look-out stool a man glowered at him and Johnson remembered the first time he had entered this place. Remembered also this man's predecessor, the deceased Phil.

A big fellow lurched suddenly in front of him. A drunk who burbled; 'It's Mack Johnson. Hey, boys, it's Mack Johnson! Welcome, Mack! Welcome.'

The man was unshaven, dirty. He lurched against Johnson and Johnson smelled liquor on his breath: and another pungent smell too, of clothes long unwashed, and stale animal sweat. He moved mechanically backwards then he drove his fist, hard, into the pit of the man's stomach. He felt it sink into a roll of soft rubbery flesh. The big feller's mouth shot open, his eyes popped. Then he doubled up, his dirty face disappeared, his clawed hands came out. Johnson avoided the scrabbling nails and rabbit-punched him viciously. His face hit the floor with a dull smack and he lay still.

Johnson went on. There was a cleared space before him now. He went forward to the bar, heard thudding feet behind him and turned swiftly. His gun seemed to leap into his hand. He leaned back against the bar. The three advancing plug-uglies pulled up short.

There was a flash of steel. Beside Johnson and above him. His gun swivelled and barked. The look-out gave a shrill cry. His derringer flashed as it spun in the air; he tumbled headlong from his stool. He rose to his knees, clutching his tingling wrist, snarling like a trapped animal.

'That was real fancy shooting, Mr Johnson,' said a voice behind the man at the bar. 'Now just drop the gun and elevate the hands.'

That was the voice he had wanted to hear. But it was in the wrong place. Too late now Johnson real-ized what a fool he had been to try and catch the little skunk in his own lair. He ought to have bided his time and got him outside. Why was he always doing things like this – things on an immediate impulse, almost trance-like while the feeling lasted? Was this the last time?

He let the gun fall. Its clatter was a harsh sound in

93

the stillness. He turned slowly to face Luke Piercy, who stood against the other side of the bar, a half-open door behind him. His little young-old face had a mocking smile, the gun in his hand was steady. He said: 'Such colossal bluff I have never seen before. What do you want here? Have you come to tell me what has happened to Slim and Marney?'

That would be the two bushwackers, thought Johnson quickly. He said: 'Their horses returned home didn't they? You should've guessed what happened to them. Your little back-shooting plot came unstuck. They weren't quite quick enough. I killed them both.'

'*You* killed them both?'

'That's what I said.'

Piercy's smile broadened. 'I've no doubt you had a dozen of your men with you at the time.'

'*You buzzard.*'

There was no passion in Johnson's tone. It was unemotional like the other man's. But the words carried and were all the more insulting for being spoken in that perfectly level voice. People there grudgingly admired Johnson's guts; were surprised at his foolhardiness (who did he think he was?) and the blood-lust rose within them. Now there would be some fireworks!

'You treacherous lying son-of-a-bitch. You know damn well you sent those two men out to get me – alone – an' in the back if need be. I'm labelling you a yellow coyote, Luke Piercy. I'm calling you out, man to man.'

The little man's smile broadened more, it

stretched his face grotesquely, but hardly seemed a part of him any more; his eyes were like little black marbles, shining strangely in the light. He looked straight at Johnson, but hardly seemed to see him, seemed to look through him – far, far, into some hell of his own creating.

'All right, boys,' he said. 'He's all yours.'

He lowered the gun, turned and went back through the door. It closed behind him.

Johnson whirled, dived for the gun on the floor. A boot swung within an inch of his lowered head, grazed his arm as it was instinctively upflung. He straightened, empty handed, to dodge another kick. Then all the men came at him at once.

He hit out right and left, feeling his fists grinding into flesh, seeing men go down before him. He charged, trying to find an opening. They tried to surround him. A fist thudded into his ear. He turned and lashed out with a foot. He felt it bite on bone, heard, with satisfaction, the cry which followed it.

He back-pedalled and, as he did so, a rocklike fist hit him in the chest and he toppled, gasping for breath. His back hit the edge of the bar with a sickening jar and the pain shot up his spine and throbbed in the recesses of his brain. He dragged air, pressing his elbows on the bar, using them as levers as he pivoted his body, swinging out with feet out-thrust viciously, driving. A big man, dark, brute-faced, received both boots in the stomach. Johnson felt the flesh cave in, crumple like a bursted paper-bag. Then the man was down, writhing in agony. And already others were taking his place.

Johnson kicked out with one foot and hit nothing. He pivoted, striking out with both fists. He struck both times. They were crowding him, nobody gave way now. A blow buffetted his shoulder, rocking him again. The bar held him up. Blows thudded on his uplifted forearms. A knee was driven into his side. He hit low savagely and a man went down, grabbing at his legs. He kicked out and the clutch slackened then went altogether.

A fist smashed through his guard, smashed clean between his eyes. His brain seemed to explode and the room spun around him. The lights a kaleidoscope, the noise a fluctuating boom. He was hanging over the bar and they were beating at him from all sides. He grabbed a bottle, like a drowning man clutching a spar. The feel of the cold glass in his hand gave him a sudden exhilaration which conquered all pain. His knuckles tightened, he gripped hard. He swung his arm around in an arc and for a moment the room was no longer spinning; there were only the mouthing faces in front of him: the bottle burst full in one of them. The man screamed and his face dissolved in blood which spattered those around him. The glass tinkled and the pungent smell of raw whiskey smote the air like another blow among all the others.

He was overwhelmed by a hail of them. Fists and boots punished him. Still the bar held him up, the feel of it against his spine just a small part of all the throbbing pain. It was coloured pain, a deep purple, and it was slowly going darker and darker and he was falling deeper into it and the lights had gone and the voices were fading and the blows were ceasing to hurt any more.

The darkness slowly lightened and he was surprised that now there were no more blows. The lights came back slowly and the rumbling voices, then one above them all, shriller than the rest.

His hands explored and found the cold brass of the footrail at the base of the bar. He levered himself to his knees. He twisted his body and let go with one hand and reached upwards. He was not aware now of what was going on around him, all his being was fixed with painful concentration on the task of getting back on his feet. His hand reached the edge of the bar and clutched there. He brought the other one up to join it. His arms felt like string and lifting his body with them was like lifting a sack of meal which was a lot too heavy for him. Finally he made it and leaned, gasping, across the bar and awareness returned to him. The lights, the sound, the shrill voice in his ears.

He turned slowly and leaned against the bar. Beside him stood Louise Praline. He could even smell her perfume now and see her so clearly that the beauty of her was like more pain. She was clad it a low-cut gown of red, shimmering, satiny stuff, and in her hands was a sawn-off shot-gun.

The sight was incongruous, but a glance at the girl's set cameo face, with the elaborately piled black hair like a head-dress above it, showed that she meant business. The men were grouped in a semi-circle a few yards away from her, half-crouching like animals waiting to pounce. Three men lay on the floor. Two were still, the other was moaning and

97

twitching feebly. Johnson felt a little proud at this evidence of his fighting prowess. He was becoming icy-cold again. Louise's voice rang in his ears – clear, like the notes of a silvery bell.

'If one of you makes a funny move I shall press the trigger. Then a whole lot of people are liable to get hurt.' She sounded icy-cold, too.

Johnson lurched forward a little, bent, and picked up his gun. He rejoined the girl. His head was spinning, but the scarred butt of the gun had a comforting feel in his hand. He looked into the hated faces, knew that with a pressure of his finger he could blow any one of them out of existence, and he felt his power returning.

'Get moving, Mack,' she said out of the corner of her mouth.

'You're coming with me. You can't stay here.'

He felt, rather than saw her shrug. 'All right,' she said.

He began to move forward and she fell into step beside him.

'Back up,' she said. 'Let us through!'

They backed, then parted. Johnson said, 'Cover the front. I'll watch the skunks.'

He swivelled until his back was to the girl. He made a slow half-circle with his gun. The pain of the bruises and cuts on his face, and all over his body, was returning now.

But his head was clear, his purpose implacable again. He just wanted one of these buzzards to move so that he could plug him dead centre. But nobody moved.

Over the heads he could see the closed door behind the bar through which Piercy had disappeared. Beside it was a bartender, probably the one who had given the alarm to the little man in the first place. He was standing still. His face was moonlike and scared-looking. He held his hands flat on top of the bar. Johnson waited with savage anticipation for the door to open. But it did not open and next thing he knew was that the night air was blowing on his back and Louise was tugging his arm and saying: 'Come on. Before somebody starts shooting.'

There was a rubbery feeling about his legs as he followed her. They ran along the boardwalk a little way. There was nobody around. They turned into an alley and behind them heard the first sounds of pursuit.

'We'll go to my rooms at Jarrold's,' said Johnson. 'Your place is too far away.'

He knew that her frame bungalow, where she lived with a negro housekeeper and her husband, the huge coachman, was on a knob behind the town.

She did not answer, she was following him now. He dropped behind.

'Give me that,' he said and took the shot-gun from her hands, which had gone suddenly lax.

'Get in front,' he said. His voice was purposeful again. His movements, too. The girl thought he must be made of iron.

The core of hardness inside her had suddenly broken, there was a fluttering in her stomach, her heart was thumping like an Indian war-drum, her legs had turned to water. She felt like she had been dealing faro for three days and nights. She was beaten, the bank was broken. That was the way she felt – much worse, very much worse.

She caught hold of his arm and held onto him. He swung her in front of him and pushed her along. As she stumbled on she looked over her shoulder. He was half-turned away from her, running with a side-ways movement. She marvelled at him being able to move like that after the beating he had received. He was like an animal, forgetting pain in a moment, his mind working now with no panic. The shot-gun was in the crook of his arm. The girl could not see his face very well but she could imagine the expression on it, an expression she had seen before and which had made her fear for what, in more ways than one, he could do to her.

A bunch of men came around the corner of the alley. She saw the muzzle of the shot-gun move around slowly, deliberately. A cry rose to her lips and was choked by the booming report, deafening between the two walls. The smoke floated back to her and through its haze she saw the men running for cover, one of them lurching forward, whimpering like a child, another one writhing soundlessly on the ground.

Her steps faltered. 'Run,' said Johnson. 'Run. That'll hold 'em for a while.' She thought she detected a note of exultation in his flat, deep voice.

But she had no time to think about it any more for she was running again and her head was thudding and there was a sick feeling of horror in the depths of her stomach. Then she was round another corner and Johnson was thudding close behind her. The shouts behind were frenzied, but dying on the wind. The wind coming across the range, from the Rio, moaning along the deserted 'backs' of El Paso.

They reached the back of Jarrold's Hotel and Johnson opened the door. His touch as he ushered the girl inside was surprisingly gentle.

They saw no one. They crossed the deserted lobby and went upstairs, where Johnson, as one of the elite, had two rooms.

She followed him and stood close behind him as he lit the lamp. She was still trembling, although she knew they were safe now. Up here it was quiet; nothing might ever have happened. Yet she did not feel safe. Could anybody feel safe while they were with Mack Johnson? knowing instinctively that his rules were not the rules of ordinary men. He had his own rules and they were lawless and desperate and untamed.

The flare of the lamp lit his bruised bloodied face and for a moment she thought she saw treacherous evil there. Then the glow became steady and, despite his wounds, he was the inscrutable Mack once more. He turned away from her suddenly, lurched across the room and collapsed on the settee.

Her fist flew to her mouth. She bit her knuckles and stood there, as if petrified, for a moment. Then as he rolled over and sat up she ran across to him.

His face was strained, pale beneath the blood which caked it. He was obviously ashamed of his sudden weakness as he drew himself up and faced her.

She sat down beside him and for a moment did not know what to do with her hands.

He said: 'Thanks, Louise.'

She said: 'I couldn't stand there and see you kicked to death. I saw it happen to a man in New Orleans.'

'Where did you get the shot-gun?'

'From behind the bar.'

'You would have used it?'

'Yes, I would have used it.'

She could feel those queer dark eyes of his fixed upon her and knew he was going to say somethinig else. He would want to know why she had taken that trouble for him, she who had seen brutality and murder before, why she had outlawed herself from her friends, her livelihood at *The Golden Hall* – for him. She could not answer those questions properly even to herself and she became suddenly panic-stricken at the thought that he might ask them. She did not regret having acted impulsively, as she did, while other women had stood by – and even been amused by the spectacle of a man being beaten to death – but that did not make any difference to her muddled feelings.

She rose suddenly. 'I'd better fix you up,' she said. 'Have you any first-aid stuff?'

'Yes,' he said. He rose, too. 'Wait a minute. There's somep'n I gotta do first.'

Before she had time to say anything else he had crossed the room and opened the door.

'I'll be right back,' he flung over his shoulder.

She heard him go along the corridor. There was

no unsteadiness about his walk now.

She heard him call, 'Jarrold!'

There was no answer but a few seconds after she heard him say, 'Oh, hallo, I didn't know you were around, Jesse.'

She heard the voice of Jesse Apgood say, 'Good grief, Mack, what happened to you? What's going on? There's a mob milling around by *The Golden Hall.*'

'I had a run in with some of Piercy's men. Get the boys together, Jesse – all of them.'

'Boss's not going to like—'

'To hell with Boss. If he's gonna like anything at all any more we've got to get moving – quickly. Are you going to get the boys, Jesse?'

'All right. I guess you know what you're doing.'

'I do. Tell 'em to come here. To the lobby.'

'All right.' There was the sound of Apgood's boot-heels clattering away down the stairs, the sound of Mack returning.

CHAPTER ELEVEN

He opened the door quickly, came in, closed it behind him.

'Where's the first-aid stuff, Mack?' she said.

He looked at her as if he was surprised to see her, as if he had forgotten her presence. There was no surprise in his eyes, but it seemed to be there in the tilt of his head, the tautness of his body. There was something in his eyes which made a shudder run through the girl's body. She knew it had no relation to her and was overwhelmingly glad of that fact.

The tautness left him and his eyes seemed to soften a little as he crossed the room towards her. He answered her question and she turned away from him and went into the bedroom.

When she returned he was sitting on the couch. She said: 'I'll get some hot water.'

'There's no time for that, Louise,' he said. 'Just use the plaster.'

She did not argue. She knew what he was going to do. She did not argue about that either. She knew it would be no use.

She sat down beside him. There was a nasty gash

above his eye. She cleaned it as best she could with a pad of cottonwool then smeared soothing ointment upon it. He did not move, did not wince. He said: 'I thought you hated me.'

'I never said I hated you.'

'No, you never did – did you? But I was one of the other side.'

'I didn't take sides. I just didn't want to start any trouble. I knew you only wanted to be friends with me so that you could pump me about Luke Piercy. You'd be surprised to learn how little I know about Piercy. I do my job – the job I came here to do – and apart from that I have nothing to do with him or his plans. I was a trusted employee. He depended on me.' She gave a little spurt of harsh laughter. 'He won't depend on me any more after this.'

'You'll be all right,' said Johnson softly.

Whatever else he was going to say was lost as a knock came upon the door. His hand moved instinctively to his gun, rested there as he said, 'Come in.'

The door opened and the big man Bullock came in quickly. He seemed agitated. He stopped dead when he saw Louise Praline. His mouth dropped open, his little eyes blinked in the light.

'Well?' said Johnson.

Still Bullock hesitated, his eyes flickering from the man to the girl and back again.

'You can talk,' said Johnson.

The words came out in a rush then. 'We did what you said, Mack. We got rid o' the horse. We was coming away from the river when a couple of fellows rode up. They looked like the marshal's two

105

deputies. They shouted. Pecos started shooting. Then we ran for it – we knew you wanted us right back. Pecos got hit. He's dead I think. I left him back there.'

'That's fine,' said Johnson. 'Just fine. It was the marshal's deputies. You know damn well it was. Did either of them get hit?'

'I dunno. I don't think so.'

'Were they behind you when you rode in?'

'No, they stopped by Pecos. I think they were bringing him in. I had a good start.'

'Did you pass anybody on your way in?'

'I passed the marshal. He was riding out. I don't think he saw me.'

Johnson thought fast. He figured that Maginnis had probably started out before the ruckus really broke loose around *The Golden Hall*.

There was another knock at the door and it opened and Jesse Apgood came in. He too stopped dead at the sight of the girl. But his smooth gambler's face showed no surprise and his voice was level as he said, 'Hallo, Louise.'

'Hallo, Jesse.'

'Well, Jesse?' said Johnson.

'Most of the boys are here and waiting. The rest are coming. There's a lot going on down the street by *The Golden Hall*. I think they're waiting for us, Mack.'

'Are they?' Johnson rose and crossed the room. He turned and looked at Louise. 'You stay here. Don't move out of the room, y'understand? I'll send Jarrold up to stand guard outside.'

'All right, Mack.'

'Come on,' he said. He had already forgotten her. The door closed behind the three of them.

The girl sat on the couch and looked at the closed door. She sat like that for a long time; she heard the men downstairs shouting; she heard Jarrold come up the stairs and halt outside the door; the only things that moved about her were her hands, which lay in her lap, the fingers clasping and unclasping, clasping and unclasping . . . .

Johnson halted halfway down the stairs, with Apgood and Bullock behind him. He spoke to the former.

'This isn't your pigeon, Jesse. You'd better get back to the tables. Keep your boys on the go, keep the people interested. We don't want a wholesale mix-up.'

'If you really think so, Mack.'

'I do. Where's Boss?'

'You know he very seldom stirs out of that office.'

'See that he don't.'

Apgood did not say anything more. He passed the two men and went down the stairs and through the throng. Johnson and Bullock remained where they were and the packed faces stared up at them.

'You've all been waiting for this,' said Johnson. 'But don't act like maniacs. Don't start shooting unless the other side does. We don't want the military here.'

'How about the Rangers, Mack?' yelled somebody.

'We'll think about them if they pop up. If anybody wants to step out they can do it right now.'

Nobody moved. More men were moving through

the doors into the lobby. Black-jacks were much in evidence. Also empty bottles. Some of the river boys and thugs from the 'Mudhole' did not seem to be carrying anything at all. But nobody was fooled. Beneath their long-tailed coats and in their capacious pockets they carried an armoury. Little lead-weighted black-jacks, razors, knives, derringers. They were past-masters in the art of the free-for-all.

Mack Johnson came down the stairs and passed among their ranks. 'Let's get going,' he said.

The motley streamed out into the street to be joined by others who, unable to get into the lobby, had been waiting outside. In a compact mass they surged down the street, the thugs, the shoulder-hitters, the thieves, the con-men, and the killers. Many of them pushed and jostled and stumbled over each other in their eagerness to be first in the fray. Others hung back and hoped there would not be any shooting.

The yelling had died; there were no voices, only a deep hum, as of a turbulent river. A river of men, a lawless river, a river of hate and blood-lust and animalism. The tramp of feet was not rhythmic, but a rushing, grinding sound.

Johnson and Bullock were in the forefront of the mob. Between them, buffeting them as he lolloped along, was a big Swede, known simply as 'Oley'. He had been a bare-knuckle prize-fighter in Chicago and had led the contingent of plug-uglies from that fabulous 'mudhole'.

He towered even over big Bullock; and the leanness of Mack Johnson seemed whip-like beside him.

His face was a battleground, his features a travesty. He was scarred and wrinkled and pitted and bulging and gnarled. His features were a map, the map of a terrain over which hundreds of engagements had been fought; white, with a nose that was spread until it was part of the cheeks and the gappy broken mouth, eyes that were sunken like tiny muddy pools, ears that were like strange twisted vegetation, the whole lit garishly by the streaming lights of the hell-hole which was El Paso.

There was another mob in the street, moving sluggishly too, lit by the lights of *The Golden Hall.* Two rivers of humanity, moving to meet each other, with tributaries both sides: fighters joining up or peaceable townspeople taking cover. The distance between the two parties was lessening when Piercy's mob drew sluggishly to a stop. Simultaneously they began to clamour; there was a sea of waving arms and the missiles began to fly through the air. Rocks, sticks, bottles, and other identifiable objects. Gruber men clutched at heads, at blood-streaming faces; staggering, falling. Their formation became V-shaped as most of the leaders sought cover along the boardwalks. Mack Johnson clutched at his shoulder. His head was down as he crouched, following Bullock to the shadows of a hitchrail. Oley cursed and clutched his stomach, swerved, and bored on like an enraged bull-buffalo.

'Rush 'em!' yelled Mack Johnson.

Boot-heels thudded, echoing, as men ran along the boardwalk on both sides, yelling, brandishing weapons. Behind them, streaming across the street, all the rest moved as the Gruber faction charged. The missiles came again but not so thick and fast. The Piercy mob were running out of ammunition. There were no guns in evidence. Nobody had been crazy enough to draw them. There was a collective roar as the two factions met, milled together with whirling limbs and garish staring faces.

Mack Johnson dodged a viciously swung bottle, which was dashed to smithereens on a hitching post behind him. He moved in, driving a sharp knee into the man's groin, not seeing his face, only hearing his hiss of pain, then hitting him again with a downward chopping blow between the shoulder-blades as he doubled. The man went flat on his face. Another man launched himself forward, tripped over the fallen body and fell headlong. Johnson heard him crash onto the sagging boards of the sidewalk. Then, moving forward, hitting out right and left, men coming for him from all sides. No panic now, triumph even, knowing he was backed up, the odds were even. Exultation, feeling fists biting into flesh. A club hit the side of his neck, the fleshy part where it met his shoulder. But he hardly felt the blow. His body was numb with bruises and he was a fighting machine. He grappled with a brawny man, got in at close quarters, drove his elbow into the man's adam's apple. The brawny man choked with agony and reeled. Johnson drew off and let loose a haymaker. The man was swept away like chaff but another took his place. Light gleamed on the wicked blade of a knife. Johnson kicked out; his boot jarred on bone and the man screamed. The knife flashed in the air and vanished in the milling crowd. The staggering man was picked up as if by a whirlwind and tossed aside. Oley, the Swede, grinned horribly and winked at Johnson. Then he turned and dived into the mass of people, using his huge fists like clubs. Johnson followed him.

Many of the Piercy men were retreating into the interior of *The Golden Hall*. Men stumbled, grabbing at each other, hitting out frenziedly. The street was one packed mass of humanity. By the doors of the saloon there was little room to fight as men were jammed together by the force of the numbers behind. A window frame caved in as a man went backwards through it. Then the double-doors crashed wide open, one of them hanging loose on a hinge. The mob burst in, like pent-up waters suddenly released.

Those in front went down with others on top of them. Furniture crashed over and was reduced to matchwood. Many men were left motionless on the floor, to be trampled by booted feet as the fighting spread out a little once more.

Little groups of men milled and beat at each other like frenzied puppets. In the street, on the board-walk, and more and more in the saloon; and even on the stairs. A man crashed from top to bottom, another fell sideways, bringing part of the banisters with him. His assailant, unable to stop himself, toppled through the gap after him. Both of them had their fall broken by the heads of those beneath.

The giant Oley chased a couple of men up the stairs. One of them turned and swung a foot, drove it

into the massive chest. Oley, his hand clutching the
sagging rail, braced himself. He shuddered beneath
the blow then bored in, head down, ape-like arms
reaching out. The man was grabbed around the
waist; as he was lifted off his feet, he beat impotently
at the giant's head, he screamed frenziedly to his
pard to help him. But the other man was already
running in panic along the corridor above.

The screaming man was heaved high above Oley's
head and tossed to the crowd below. His hurtling
body took two men like ninepins with it. The three of
them landed in a tangled heap amid the wreckage of
a small table. That one of them belonged to his own
side, even if he had known it, would have meant little
to the giant. He was fighting for the sheer lust of
fighting, trance-like, a perfect animal. He was already
in pursuit along the landing after the other man. He
hated any yellow dog to escape him.

The man seized a chair which stood outside one of
the doors. He flung it along the passage. Oley got his
legs entangled in it and fell with a crash which made
the building vibrate. The man ran on, reached the
door at the end of the passage, the door which led to
the back-stairs. He lifted the latch, jerked at the door.
It was locked. He turned frenziedly, looking about.
Oley was charging for him again like a mad bull-
buffalo. The man grabbed the handle of the nearest
door in sight, flung it open. He hardly heeded the
screams as the girls, who had been lying low in their
dressing-room, scattered on all sides. The dancing
girls, who wore tights, got away the quickest. Some of
them crouched at the back of the room, others

darted past the man and ran down the passage. Oley went through them as if they were a mere slightly-irritating bunch of mosquitoes.

The lady dealers, the percentage girls, were hampered by their long skirts. One of them went sprawling, getting herself entangled in her frills and furbelows. The panic-stricken man, as eager to find hiding as any of them, did a nose-dive over the top of her. He rose, darted forward again. A percentage girl with more spunk than the rest of them smote him on the head with a brass candlestick. A silly look came over his face; he bent at the knees, then pitched forward.

The percentage girl, a black Irish Amazon, spat on her hands and took a firmer grip on the candlestick as Oley came through the door. The giant stopped dead, he was mortally afraid of female kind. His little eyes ranged the room.

'Come on in, yez big ape,' chanted the Irish girl and brandished her candlestick.

· Oley's eyes fell on his fallen foe, then shifted to the girl. She advanced threateningly. Others, heartened, began to hurl shrill abuse at the giant.

'Ay bag yo' pardon, ma'am,' he said and turned and ran. The candlestick hit the edge of the door behind him.

He charged on and did not stop running until he reached the bottom of the stairs. He dived once more into the fray and vented his spleen on the nearest heads.

By now the place was a shambles. All the ornate mirrors were shattered, there was not a pane of glass left in any of the windows, one of the chandeliers

113

hung crazily in danger of falling any moment, the mob fought and tumbled over jagged spars of wood and fantastically shaped objects which had once been furniture. Only the sturdy gambling tables remained intact, and most of these had been over-turned. A roulette wheel spun crazily as dozens of feet kicked it, playing cards and dice were trampled upon, 'chips' were scattered like coloured snow. The place reeked of sweating human flesh and the fumes of liquor from dozens of broken bottles.

Mack Johnson, bleeding profusely from the face and limping as he moved, found himself in the middle of a cleared space and stopped and looked around him. He saw Bullock go down as a bottle burst on his head. Blood stained the boards as he fell. Johnson flung himself forward. The man who had wielded the bottle went down before the fury of the sudden attack. Johnson leapt on top of him, driving his knees into his chest. Something snapped; the man screamed once, and lay still.

Johnson rose, took a cursory look at Bullock. The man was merely unconscious. Johnson looked around him again. He saw Oley throwing men away from him right and left. He saw another of his men standing on the bar and wielding a long piece of wood like a flail. He saw another standing on the musician's dais, kicking out at any enemy head which came within easy reach. The Piercy men were being beaten and their stronghold pulled to pieces around their ears.

Johnson thought about Piercy: he had either run for it or was skulking like a rat somewhere. He wiped a torn sleeve across his bleeding face and started forward once more. A man got in his way and he struck out viciously without pausing in his stride, feeling the shock speed up his arm as his fist connected, seeing the man go down, stepping over him, going on. He vaulted the bar and the man wielding the flail grinned at him.

Johnson went through the door behind the bar and closed it behind him. In the passage there was nobody, there was nothing, the tumult came to him but dimly through the thickness of the door. There was carpet beneath his feet and he traversed it on tiptoes, his hand on his gun. Things were a little too quiet. He had an idea somebody was watching him, and his skin began to crawl, half expecting the impact of a bullet, the flash, the crashing report.

He drew his gun with a flick of his wrist, flattened himself against the wall, went along it slowly. He reached two doors, one each side of the passage. There was a thin thread of light at the bottom of the one on the left-hand side. Johnson stood still and listened.

He heard no sound except the muffled tumult of the battle, like the booming of distant surf. He moved one foot forward slowly until his feet were braced apart. He held his gun ready, the barrel uptilted a little. He looked up and down the empty passage. He reached out with his free hand and grasped the knob of the door. He twisted it – he flung the door open with a crash. Nothing happened and he bent and went in, crouching, his face predatory, his gun uplifted. The room was empty.

He straightened up, looking around him. He realized he was in Piercy's office. The room was in disorder. Papers were strewn about on the desk; some of them were torn or crumpled. It looked like the rat, in his panic, had grabbed everything of value, and then run like hell.

Johnson closed the door behind him and crossed the room to the desk. Then he stiffened. His foot made a hollow sound, loud in the stillness, as it met the desk. He bent forward.

Luke Piercy lay at the back of his swivel-chair, which was half-turned away from the desk. He lay on his back and grinned up at Johnson. His throat was cut from ear to ear.

Johnson went around the desk and bent over him.

The dead man's clothes were crumpled. His fancy vest was wrinkled up under his armpits. His trouser pockets had been turned inside out. Johnson wondered what kind of a haul the murderous buzzard had gotten – from this room, from this grinning dummy which bore no resemblance to life any more.

The blood was shiny and slick. Piercy had not been dead long. Johnson straightened up again and looked around the room. Then he turned and retraced his steps. He opened the door and passed through. He was making for the back of the saloon when the tumult out front was suddenly redoubled in intensity. He heard a shot, then the door at the end of the passage flew open and men tumbled through.

'*The law! The Rangers!*'

CHAPTER TWELVE

Louise Praline sat on the couch. Sat on the edge of the couch with her fists taut upon her knees. How long she had been there like that she did not know. The rioting down at *The Golden Hall* came to her as a subdued clamour, rising and falling. By the sound of it she tried to judge how the battle was going. She heard Jarrold shouting to somebody downstairs but could not make out what he said. She did not think of rising and going to the door to enquire how things were going. She knew she was powerless to help now, no matter what happened. She sat on the couch and listened and waited.

She no longer felt like the hard-boiled, poker-faced Louise Praline of El Paso, the arrogant, the unapproachable; that had been her pose for the last few years, the armour with which she cloaked her self-respect; the armour behind which she hid her loneliness, her awareness that her success, such as it was, had turned to dust and ashes in her heart.

She was a frightened young girl again. On a Mississippi river-boat dealing cards to hard-faced men. Beside her father, shabby, shifty-eyed: a small-time sharper. Only a faint memory in her mind of a mother who had been gentle and lady-like, of a farm clean and prosperous. The farm gambled away, the mother dead from weakness and a broken heart.

After that there had been a long succession of river-side towns, all of them alike in their varying degrees of squalor and wickedness. Dirty rooms in dirty boarding-houses; the attentions of dirty men; her father rolling and mumbling and stinking of liquor. Fleeing in the dead of night because they could not pay their rent; catching the river-boat on the stinking mudbanks in the cold light of the dawn. Sleeping in low cabins amid the smells of oil and bilge. The wealthy times, the rare happy times; the big gambling halls, the dancing, the faultlessly-dressed men and the beautifully dressed women; the dresses she had worn to emulate their grandeur; the downward slide, the liquor, everything sold to scrape and exist; the river-boats again.

Then came the night. The night in Memphis, hell-hole of gambling and vice on the banks of the Mississippi. At first it was a night very much like many other nights. Nick, her father, had gone out to spend his last few dollars on drink and gambling, to lose all or win some more. He had left Louise alone in the dirty rooming-house bedroom, partitioned off by a curtain, in which they had both slept the night before. She passed away the time by playing solitaire, for cards and dice were in a way almost as much a passion with her as they were with her father. Although she bowed to their enchantment she hoped they would never coarsen and demoralise her as they had Nick.

She played all night, dropping to sleep over her cards, waking and looking at the clock and running into the passage. But dawn came and still no Nick and she drank black coffee to stimulate herself and went out into the cold dusty streets to look for him.

She did not find him. But others did and it was bright noon when the law brought her the news. Nick had been fished out of the river with three bullets in his back, his pockets rifled and torn apart. Last night he had broken the bank at Memphis's biggest 'gambling-hell'. One of his murderers had been caught and shot to death and some of the money recovered. There was no clue to the identity of the others.

She took the two thousand dollars they gave her. Some of it went towards the cost of burying her father in Memphis Boot Hill. It was just after the funeral that she met Pattie, the motherly negro woman, and her massive husband, Satch. When she left Memphis she took them with her. They went West with the railroad. To the boom-towns, the end-of-track towns, where Louise dealt faro, guarded always by the mighty, implacable Satch and mothered by Pattie, his wife. It was in Waco that she met Luke Piercy. She joined his troupe and came to El Paso . . . .

Louise started as she heard the tap-tap of hurrying footsteps in the passage and the gruff voice of Jarrold speaking again. Her thoughts fled away from her and she was back in the lamplit room with the ominous noises coming to her from the distance and the sharper noises directly outside.

119

She heard Jarrold talking gruffly. Then the sound of a girl's voice and more footsteps. Then the door opened and Lucy Studamiere came in.

She stopped dead when she saw Louise. Her blue eyes were wide, she looked agitated. She said quickly: 'What are you doing here? What's happening? Where's Mack?'

Of a sudden Louise Praline was the hard-boiled, arrogant El Paso gambling woman once more.

'Don't you know where Mack is? I thought you knew all about him.'

Lucy did not seem to notice the implied insult. She shut the door behind her. She said: 'I've been at the theatre. Somebody ran in shouting. The place emptied. I came here. It looks like there is a riot going on down by *The Golden Hall.*'

'There is. The Gruber gang have attacked the Piercy gang.' Louise smiled thinly. Her beautiful face was cold and white.

'Mack's leading the Gruber men?'

'Yes, Mack's leading them,' said Louise. 'I'm waiting for him.'

The other girl stood aimlessly before the door. They faced each other, one standing, one sitting. In some ways they were very much alike. They both spoke with a Southern brogue. Their names were very similar. Good old-fashioned Southern names. *Louise. Lucy.* Their last names, too, had that French sound so often found in Southern surnames. *Praline. Studamiere.* They might have been friends. Both beautiful. Both used to public acclaim. One dark, the other blonde . . . But there was a man between them and, in their different ways, they knew it now. The one could put only one construction on the other's enigmatic smile and, beaten and bitter, was turning to the door when it opened and Mack Johnson came in.

Both girls gave exclamations of horror at the sight of him.

'Lucy,' he said. 'What are you doing here?'

'I was worried about you,' she said. Her voice was barely audible.

Then she drew herself up. Her voice rang by contrast as she said, 'I'm going now.'

He looked from one to the other of the two girls and his bleeding face told them nothing. Lucy's eyes were bright as if she felt his pain for him. But she went past him.

'Lucy,' he said. 'I—'

The door banged in his face. That same face was expressionless as he turned it towards Louise. The blood had dried in streaks upon it. He looked rather like a painted drug-store Indian and the girl had a sudden hysterical desire to laugh. Then she saw the way his arm dangled and she gasped and rose and ran across to him. She touched his shoulder tentatively.

'Sit down, Mack. Let me have a look at that arm.'

He passed her without a word. His body was taut, he seemed to be walking on the balls of his feet. When he reached the couch his body went slack, he pivoted around and sagged. His head went back.

He straightened up when she reached him. He said: 'Piercy's dead. Somebody took advantage of the

121

ruckus and stabbed him and robbed him. The Texas
Rangers turned out, guns an' all; they're patrolling
the streets now like a bunch of nighthawks. I'll say
somep'n for those boys: they don't scare easy.'

She felt a faint sense of horror at the news of Luke
Piercy's death. He had been so self-sufficient, so arrogant, so sure of himself. She felt relief that the
Rangers were here. Their name carried power,
people feared the force they stood for, a force which
was growing all the time, loyal to justice, but implacable.

These thoughts brushed the surface of her mind
but most of her concentration was fixed on the task
of rolling up Mack's sleeve. She revealed the purple
bruise, stretching from his elbow almost to the point
of his shoulder.

'Somebody hit me with a chair,' he said.

She used ointment and bandages and trussed up
the arm. 'Good job it ain't my gun arm,' said
Johnson.

She felt a chill at the words, a sudden revulsion
from him. This was replaced, however, perversely, by
a flood of tenderness.

'Let me fix your face,' she said. 'Your poor face –
it has been knocked about lately.'

'It sure has.'

There was a knock on the door. A voice called,
'Mack !'

'Come in,' said Johnson.

The door opened and Jesse Apgood entered.

'Hell's popping,' he said. 'Boss wants to see you,
Mack.' He stopped. 'You hurt?'

'Nothin' to speak of. Got a cigarette? I lost my "makings" in the ruckus.'

Apgood took out a packet of cigarettes. He crossed the room.

Johnson took one and said 'Thanks.' He leaned back on the couch. Apgood struck a match and lit up for him, then lit one for himself.

'Boss's hopping mad.'

'Is he?'

'You coming along, Mack?'

'When I'm ready.'

Apgood half turned, hesitated. Then he said, 'I'll carry on,' and made for the door. It closed behind him.

Johnson rose and crossed the room. His weariness had left him. Louise said: 'Mack, I've got to fix your face.'

'It'll keep,' he said with unconscious humour.

He took out his gun, spun the cylinder, checked it, reholstered it. Frozen-faced, the girl watched him. He turned his head and looked at her. He said: 'Stay here, Louise.'

'All right,' she said. There was so much more she could have said. But she knew it was best left unspoken: it would not make any difference either way.

A sudden wild impulse came over her. She ran across the room and flung her arms around his neck. She kissed him and then he was away from her and had opened the door. It closed and she was left staring at it a little stupidly. She heard his footsteps along the passage. Then they stopped. She heard him talking, a gruff voice answering. She could not hear the words. She went back to the couch and sat down, trance-like, waiting again.

In the passage Johnson met Jarrold, keeper of the hotel. Johnson said: 'You've got a spare room, haven't you, Mike?'

'Yeh.'

'Fix it up for Miss Praline. Give her everything she wants.'

'I thought she was—'

'She's on our side now,' interrupted Johnson curtly. 'She saved my life a while ago – back in *The Golden Hall*. Do as I say, Mike, I'll take full responsibility.'

'Will you tell Boss?'

'Yes, I'll tell Boss. I'm goin' to see him right now.'

Johnson turned away. Over his shoulder he said: 'Don't you wish this place was your own, Mike?'

'Shore do.'

Johnson went down the stairs and across the lobby into the street. There was an air of brooding quiet over everything. There was no wide flash of light from *The Golden Hall*. Men paced slowly along the boardwalks on both sides. Johnson passed one of them whose face was turned towards him but whose eyes were hidden under a wide pulled-down hat-brim. As he went on Johnson could feel those eyes boring into his back.

He reached the theatre and turned into the alcove. He stood there for a moment. The footsteps stopped. He took out his key and unlocked the door and went along the passage. Monk came round the corner to meet him, a gun glinting in his hand.

'Oh, it's you, Mack,' he said. He sounded sullen; he watched Johnson warily out of his little eyes. Johnson went on, crossed the lush carpet amid the shaded lights, knocked on the door, opened it and went in.

Jesse Apgood whirled, hand flying inside his coat. Boss Gruber looked up from his desk.

'Relax, Jesse,' said Johnson.

Boss looked at Apgood and said, 'You can go now, Jesse. You know what to do.'

Apgood seemed to hesitate for a fraction of time. Then, without saying anything he quitted the place.

Boss began to write something on a pad before him. He did not say anything more. Johnson sat down. He looked at the top of the fat man's yellow hairless head. Drive your fist into it and maybe it would burst like a rotten watermelon.

'Was there something you wanted to tell me, Boss?' he said.

Boss looked up. His blubbery lips stretched in his toothless grin. There was no emotion behind it and his little eyes were almost hidden in their pouches of fat. He said, in a toneless rumble: 'You're finished in El Paso, Mack.'

'What makes you think that, Boss?'

'You acted too fast. You tried to tear the place apart. I hadn't got that far with my plans, Mack. Why did you do it?'

'What are you moaning about? Piercy's dead, isn't he? There's nobody in your way now.'

'Except maybe you, Mack. You won't take orders

from any man will you?'

'If we hadn't attacked when we did the Piercy mob might have got here first. You wouldn't've liked that would you?'

'I didn't want Piercy finished off that way.'

'I didn't kill him. You don't think I killed him do you?'

'You went out back. I know men who saw you go out back. You were seen coming out of Piercy's room.'

'Maybe I should have killed him if somebody hadn't beaten me to it. But I wouldn't have knifed him. I'd've broken his scrawny neck.'

'You're finished in El Paso, Mack.'

'Make a song up about it. You're cagey now you're finally top dog in the town, now the opposition's been squashed, you want to stay top: you're scared of what I might be able to do to you if I turned nasty.'

'I can't do much with a pack of Rangers in the street. It's fatal to meddle with a troop of Rangers, Mack. But I'm not frightened of you. You're finished. You killed Piercy or had him killed and I want no part of it.'

Johnson leaned forward in his seat. 'If I killed Piercy like you say I did what's to stop me killing you the same way?'

'I've got a derringer in my hand under this desk and it's pointing right at your stomach.' Boss's grin widened. He brought his hand up and the wicked muzzle of the little steel-plated gun winked at Johnson.

'The theatre's full of my trusted men; men who

126

have not fallen under your influence. They know what to do if you start any trouble. What you do when you get outside this room is no concern of mine. But you're no longer in my employ.'

'Was I ever in your employ?' Johnson rose and made for the door.

Boss called him and he turned. The fat man said: 'Incidentally – I have recently been honoured with a visit from the marshal. We've called a truce. I have promised to hold the reins on the – er – sporting element of El Paso and the marshal is going to talk turkey to the Rangers. He does not fool me. He's a mighty smart man.'

'And I'm to be your scapegoat—' Johnson turned again. Over his shoulder he said, 'Watch yourself, Boss.' Then he went through the door.

CHAPTER THIRTEEN

He passed Monk in the passage without looking at him. The big man had sheathed his gun but his hand was very near it. He watched Johnson as if he were a mad dog, watched him until he went through the door in the passage, until it closed behind him.

Johnson stood on the boardwalk outside the theatre; he stood immobile, he seemed to be sniffing the air. The steady feet went tramp-tramp on both sides of the street; from the direction of *The Spinning Wheel* came the sounds of music and voices. The bawdy life of El Paso was going on much the same as usual; Luke Piercy and *The Golden Hall* were forgotten.

Mack Johnson did not look at the lean silent men who passed him. He walked to the end of the street and stopped finally at a dark barn-like frame structure. At the side of it was a corral. A few horses jostled there. He went around the side of the building. A faint glow of light escaped from a curtained window. He rapped on a door.

Footsteps shuffled inside. A gruff voice said, 'Who is it?'

'Mack Johnson.'

A chain rattled. The door was opened a crack. A pencil of light escaped, glinting on the barrel of a gun. The man's face above it was hidden in shadow.

'You don't trust anybody do you, Mose?' said Johnson.

The door opened wider. 'Come in, Mack,' said the man. 'Have a drink.'

'Wal, thanks, Mose. What I really came for was to buy a horse.' He followed the man into the shack.

The man turned. He was big and very hairy. He tucked his gun into the waistband of his trousers.

'What happened to the hoss you had?'

'It was stolen.'

'Yeh?' The man guffawed. 'Fancy Mack Johnson havin' his hoss stolen.'

Something like a smile crossed the other's battered face. 'Where's that drink?'

Mose took out a bottle and poured them a couple of mugsful of the fiery stuff. He said: 'My, your face is purty. That must have been some ruckus.' He shook his head sadly. 'I got there a mite too late. I nearly tangled with a Ranger.'

Johnson knew that Mose was too fond of his own skin to have taken any risks. He was buttering up to Johnson now because of the latter's status with the Gruber mob. Johnson wondered what Mose's reactions would be had he known that, at present, the status was at rock-bottom.

They had another couple of drinks then went outside. Johnson selected a horse from those in the corral, a big black, and paid for it with a roll of bills he took from his body-belt.

He said 'So long' to Mose and led the horse out of the corral and down the street. His steps were lagging now; he had taken a beating and he felt deadly tired.

He led the horse into Pueblo's livery-stable. The fat Mexican came bustling out of the shadows, then stopped dead when he saw who his visitor was.

'*Señore* Johnson,' he said. 'You found your horse? You found your horse, uh?'

'No, Pueblo, I haven't found my horse. I've had to buy another one.'

'I could not help. They come and take.'

'All right. Did they take the saddle as well?'

'No, they did not.' The fat Mexican sounded surprised.

Johnson's face creased in the darkness. Pueblo said, 'You want the saddle?'

'Nope, just look after it for me. And look after this horse, too. I might be needing him soon so don't let him get stolen.'

'No, *Señore Johnson*. No.' Pueblo bustled forward to take the lead-rope. He was overjoyed at being let down so lightly.

Johnson left him and went out into the street again, along the boardwalk to Jarrold's Hotel. He crossed the lobby and climbed the stairs. On the landing outside her door stood Lucy Studamiere. With her was Jesse Apgood, who seemed to be talking urgently. They both turned their heads as Johnson came up the stairs. Then the girl said something and went into her room. She closed the door and Apgood was left standing in the passage.

Johnson ignored him and went on to his own room. He opened the door and stepped inside. Louise rose from the couch and ran to him. She clung to him and he could feel her trembling.

He said: 'Didn't Jarrold find you a room?'

'Jarrold? I haven't seen him. I've been here all the time.'

He led her back to the couch and sat her down. Then he went out into the passage and called. 'Mike!'

Jesse Apgood was down in the lobby now. He looked up. Mike Jarrold came through a door, looked up too, hesitated. Apgood jerked his head and said something; Johnson could not hear what it was.

'Mike,' he called. 'Come on up.'

Two other men came through the door behind the hotel-keeper. Johnson recognized them immediately. They were two of Boss Gruber's particular pets. Two quick-shooting gents from the Barbary Coast who carried their guns in shoulder-holsters. The three men began to climb the stairs. Jesse Apgood stood still for another moment, then brought up the rear.

Johnson pressed his hands on the balcony rail and watched them. His eyes did not flinch. When they reached the top of the stairs he said: 'I asked you to give Miss Praline a room, Mike.'

Jarrold said suddenly, 'I've had orders not to.'

'Whose orders?'

'Boss's. He sent Jesse round to tell me.'

'He did, uh?'

'That's right, Mack,' came Apgood's voice at the rear.

131

'An' I suppose you told him Miss Praline was here. An' all the rest of the dirt.'

'I'm your friend, Mack. I got you into this. I—'

'I know – you saved my life. But you had your purpose. Boss wanted me. Now Boss don't want me any more – uh? Now things are changed.'

Jarrold said, 'Boss says you've got to go tonight, Mack. He said I was to rent your room to somebody else.'

Johnson faced the four men. The hotel-keeper moved to one side, making room for the two gunmen. Their eyes were cold, watchful. They knew the merciless prowess of this man in front of them.

He looked from one to the other. He said: 'So I could draw. I could get both of you. But you'd get me – or mebbe your friend, Jesse, would. Boss 'ud like that.'

Apgood moved slowly forward. He was bolder now, arrogant, master of the situation. 'You've got the wrong slant, Mack.'

'Have I? I go – you take over where I left off. You'd like that wouldn't you, Jesse – in lots o' ways.'

'You've got the wrong slant, Mack,' said Apgood monotonously. His face was smooth. He moved a little further forward.

'Stay still, Jesse. You make me nervous.'

Apgood stiffened. He said: 'Are you going to do as Mike says, Mack? It'll save a lot of trouble.'

'All right, Jesse.' He half turned. Then he said, 'I'll see you boys.' His tone was flat. He turned his back on them and went along the passage to his room.

The four men stood motionless until the door closed behind him. Then Apgood jerked his thumb and they went downstairs.

They gathered in the lobby. Apgood said, 'All of you stay within call. If he doesn't come down soon we'll have to go and fetch him.'

'You can go if you like,' said Jarrold sullenly. 'I'm staying in my kitchen. I ain't aimin' to die just yet. Anyway, I like Mack,' he added defiantly.

'Boss isn't going to like to hear such things,' said Apgood silkily.

Jarrold did not say anything more. He turned and stomped off to his kitchen. The door banged behind him.

Up in the room Johnson was packing things into a valise and talking at the same time.

'Looks like me an' you are outcasts o' the storm, honey, two of a kind. The snorting gentry of El Paso ain't got any use for us any more.'

'You can come up to my place,' said the girl softly. 'There's plenty of room up there. Satch and Pattie are there, too.'

He turned and looked at her. 'People 'ull talk about you,' he said. 'Me – I don't care. But they'll talk about you – alone up there with me an' two negroes.'

'Does it matter now? Outcasts you said: two of a kind.'

'No. I guess it don't matter any more.' Johnson tossed a short blanket coat across to her. 'Here – put this on.'

She put it around her shoulders. He clapped his

sombrero on his head, picked up his valise and his rifle.

'Come on,' he said.

She followed him out of the room and down the stairs. There was nobody around. They reached the lobby. Upstairs a door opened. Johnson turned his head quickly. He was just in time to see Lucy's piquant face looking down at him. Then the door closed. Louise caught hold of his arm as they went through the doors.

They walked along the street and on up the hill until the lights were behind them. The wind whipped at them up here and the ground was uneven beneath their feet.

Johnson said: 'I don't envy you rattling up and down here in that carriage.'

'I don't mind it. Satch is a good driver. I like living up here. It's nice to come up here of nights in the freshness of the wind after being in a stuffy, smoky place all day. This is what I've always wanted - ever since I was a kid - a house on a hill.' She laughed harshly and the wind caught the sound and played with it a while and tossed it away.

'Well I got it,' she said. 'My house on the hill. Seems like it's all I have got right now . . .'

'I guess it's my fault, Louise!'

'No, it's not, don't be apologetic, Mack. It isn't like you to be that way. I hate you when you're apologetic. I wanted shaking out of it. I couldn't have gone on like this. I'm not bad, Mack – not really bad.'

'I know that, Louise. But I am. Don't think too much of me – I'm real bad.'

'No, Mack. Don't say that!' The girl became inarticulate, clinging tightly to his arm.

They were like children lost in the darkness, talking nonsense, trying to reassure each other. They got nearer to the large frame house on the hill and lights winked to greet them. As they approached the verandah a large figure loomed up before them. There was a dull glint of steel.

'Satch doesn't take any chances,' said Louise softly. 'He worships me. He'd do anything. He'd kill for me if I asked him to.'

'Who's that with y', Miss Louise?'

'It's a friend, Satch.'

They stepped on the verandah and the big negro moved aside.

Johnson saw that he held a sawn-off shot-gun. He wondered whether it was from this man that Louise had learned how to handle one of those weapons so aptly.

The door opened and a fat negress stood there. Her face shone like ebony, her eyes and teeth sparkled.

'Youse home, honey! We's been so worried. The fighting down in town an' all!'

'Mr Johnson took good care I didn't come to no harm.'

'Mr Johnson?' The voice was a little suspicious. The woman blocked the doorway. Behind Johnson her husband with the shot-gun stood big and silent.

Pattie said: 'Satch was coming down with the carriage but I said best wait a bit – nobody's go'na harm Miss Louise.'

135

'I was jes' coming,' rumbled Satch. His wife glared at him and his voice died away into mumbling.

Then Louise started forward and Pattie stepped aside and said, 'Good evening, Mistuh Johnson' as they passed her. It seemed like she had finally made up her mind about the lean young man who had brought her mistress home.

Johnson sat down in a rocking-chair beside the scrub-table in the spacious kitchen. The motherly negro woman threw up her hands in horror at the sight of his face.

'My,' she said. 'You wants some warm water on that and some salve.'

Satch came in and propped his shot-gun in the corner. He moved very lightly for such a big man. He said: 'I'll make some cawfee.'

Johnson rested his elbow on the table, his chin on his hand. The room seemed to be slowly swimming around him. He could not even see the lovely face of Louise properly. For a moment it wasn't her face, pale, cold, framed by raven-black hair, any more, but another one, blue-eyed, piquant, with locks like spun gold. *Louise* . . . *Lucy* . . . they were just women. Women were not good for a man. Women brought about weakness. Mack Johnson could not afford weakness. Now less than ever he could not afford weakness. *Lucy* . . . *Louise.* Names so much alike . . . just names . . . Just women . . . Just faces floating in a haze.

He heard a deep voice from afar, far away say, 'Drink this, suh,' and a cold glass was pressed between his fingers. He raised it to his lips, mechanically, tilted it.

It was raw whiskey. It tingled on his lips and made a ball of heat in his stomach.

It was followed by a scalding cup of coffee and Johnson began to sit up and look alive. He was able to bathe his own wounds – marvelling the while at the place to which the girl had brought him. It was a miniature edition of the ornate mansions he had seen in the 'Nob Hill' districts of some of the larger Western 'boom' cities.

Later Satch led him to a room which held a four-poster bed with the appearance of a covered wagon. To a man used to sleeping on boarding-house beds – or the hard ground – the clinging feather mattress was a strange and disturbing object. After a period of tossing and turning which revealed to him the location of every one of the myriad bruises on his aching body he dozed off into a troubled sleep. The hard lump of the gun under his pillow had a more comforting feel than anything else.

He awoke suddenly and the sun was streaming through the window and there was somebody else in the room. His hand went under the pillow, gripped the warm butt of the .45, then rested there as Satch advanced on the bed with a tray. Steam curled upwards from a huge mug of coffee and there were corn biscuits too. Johnson removed his hand.

'Morning, suh,' said the huge negro.

'Morning, Satch.' Emotions chased each other across Johnson's mind – less phlegmatic than usual. The black face which looked down upon his was more inscrutable than his own. What thoughts were going through Satch's mind? What did he think of this saw-toothed shark his mistress had netted? Louise had said that he would kill for her – Johnson looked at the bulging shoulders, the huge hands – it was a chilling thought.

He took the coffee and biscuits and watched the negro pad away until the door closed behind him. He moved like a huge cat and made no sound at all.

They had breakfast in the high panelled dining-room seated one at each end of the long table. Afterwards, despite Louise's pleas, Johnson insisted on going down the hill into the town. He would not allow her to go with him.

She watched him from a window. He minced down the trail a little awkwardly in his high-heeled boots. His head was high, his back straight, but his arms did not swing: they hung at his side, the hands a little way away from his body.

The sun etched the dark leanness of his figure as it got smaller and smaller. Louise had an impulse to run after him: she felt that she was seeing him for the last time; but finally he disappeared and still she remained there.

He had not looked back once and he had vanished into the haze which hung over El Paso. She turned away from the window. Aimlessly, clenching and unclenching her hands.

CHAPTER FOURTEEN

The town drowsed. There were few people in El Paso Street. Down at the railhead a train began to shunt. Men leaned on tie-rails, on posts and fences and eyed Johnson with speculative eyes. One or two spoke; Johnson acknowledged their salutations with a flip of his hand.

He did not look much different than usual. There was no air about him of a beaten man – an outcast.

There were strangers in the street. Lean, hard-eyed men with lowslung guns. The Lone-star Rangers were still on patrol. They lounged and smoked and spat in the dust but their eyes were watchful. They looked Johnson up and down indifferently, but they did not fool him. He was making for Pueblo's place when a man hailed him.

Others looked in the same direction as Mack Johnson turned slowly. Pete and Charlie, the marshal's two deputies, stood eyeing him, their thumbs hooked into their belts. He did not move so they began to come slowly towards him. Townsfolk moved from the immediate vicinity. Rangers drew nonchalantly closer.

Mack Johnson's hand moved upwards. The two deputies paused in their strides, their eyes dark and shifty. Johnson took the stub of a cigarette from his mouth and flipped it into the middle of the street.

The deputies came closer. Charlie said: 'The marshal 'ud like to see you, Mack.'

Johnson moved then. He moved in between the two men. The three of them went along the boardwalk and disappeared into the marshal's office. El Paso Street fell once more into an uneasy drowse.

Steve Maginnis sat behind his desk with his thumbs hooked in the armholes of his vest. His huge silver watchchain was taut across his broad chest. Johnson strode across the room and seated himself opposite him. He did not say anything.

Maginnis regarded him from under lowered lids. There was a bleak smile on his face beneath the luxuriant black moustache. He said: 'Good morning, Mack – or should I call you Chipper?'

'Should you call me Chipper? I don't get you, Steve.'

'You get me all right.'

'Explain yourself. Tell me another of your little stories.'

Maginnis shrugged slightly. He looked around him. Charlie sat on the bench against the wall. Pete was leaning against the jamb of the closed door.

'Well, if that's what you want – all right. First of all look at this – it's a back number of a New Mexico news-sheet.'

140

Johnson took it and glanced down the front page. He said nothing. He did not even look interested. Maginnis went on talking.

'As you can see, most of the paper is taken up by a report of a big bank robbery in Santa Fe. The bandits got away with almost half-a-million in gold. It was the slickest bank hold-up for years: the bandits didn't even have to kill anybody. There is a description of the leader of the gang, a young man known as Chipper McGee. The description fits you like a glove, Mack – except for that bit of fuzz on your top lip, which I believe you've only sported since you got to El Paso.'

Johnson said nothing. Maginnis brought up another paper from beneath the desk. 'This is a week older than the other one,' he said as he tossed it across. 'It tells of how a posse caught up with the bandits and there was a gun battle. Three of the posse were killed. Two of the bandits were killed and one captured. The others got away – in separate directions. It is thought that Chipper McGee, who had the bulk of the gold, was alone and he was making for the border. It is quite probable that his pardners, knowing he had the pay-off, would purty soon be on his tail. I'm inclined to back up this theory myself . . .'

'You sure are a purty speechifier, Steve,' said Johnson tonelessly. As he spoke both the deputies stiffened. Nothing happened.

Maginnis smiled. 'I've got a theory o' my own, too. Would you like to hear it?'

'Sure. I've got all the time in the world. Go ahead.'

141

'Chipper McGee did make for the border. He knew that, once on the other side, he would at least be safe from the posse for the time being, as their power ceased when they reached the divide and – the way things are in the West at present it would be quite a while before they could get the federal law on the case. Now, Chipper was almost at the divide when his horse gave out on him. He had to get another one or he was sunk. If the posse did not catch up with him his pards might. They didn't have to wait on no federal law. His luck was in, however: an old-timer came along driving a wagon and team. Chipper shot one of the horses, overturned the wagon, pitched out the old man and knocked him unconscious. Then he took the best horse and, hoping to throw his pursuers off the trail, rode along the banks of the river and finally forded it near here.' The marshal paused, a mockingly thoughtful expression on his face. Johnson looked at him and said nothing.

'One thing I forgot. I believe that somewhere along the line – maybe this side, maybe just over the other side – Chipper stashed the loot, meaning to go back and pick it up later when the heat had blown off. Ultimately he came to El Paso and, with his undeniable talents, soon became ramrod of a bunch of killers, plug-uglies, gamblers and prostitutes. Maybe it wasn't really what he wanted – maybe it was somewhat of a come-down for the great Chipper McGee – but I guess he figured it would serve his purpose. I guess he figured that if his pards did catch up with him, with all the thugs he now had at his beck and call he could soon get rid of them.

142

Then all he had to do was go back and pick up the gold and light out for places new. It all sounds so damned easy, don't it, Chipper?'

'Mack'll do for the present. Go on talking. Make some more stories up.'

'Stories, yeh. But now I'm gonna tell you a true one.' Maginnis jerked a thumb over his shoulder.

'Back in the cells we've got your side-kick Pecos. Apart from a busted shoulder he's all right an' he's been singing like a bird. He told us that you sent him an' Bullock down to the Rio to sink a dead horse – which turned out to be Miss Lucy Studamiere's paint.'

'All right, so it was. Lucy was with me when the two Piercy men dry-gulched us. I just wanted to keep the girl's name out of it that's all.'

'Very commendable, Chipper. Very commendable indeed.'

'Cut out this Chipper business,' Johnson almost snarled. His mask had broken for a moment. The two deputies moved, then, at a sign from the marshal, became still again.

'All right, if it pleases you. Keep still – you make my men nervous. To continue: Pecos told us something else; about a horse they stole for you from Pueblo's stable, your own horse. They hid it in the old mine workings. It isn't there any more, Charlie fetched it early this morning. It's out back o' the jail now. There's a brand on its flank – a cross and a six – just like that old rancher described it.'

'Even if I stole that horse – an' you said yourself it happened over the river outside of your jurisdiction

143

– that don't prove I'm this Chipper McGee.'

'You're right – it doesn't. And, even if it did, I'd have no legal right to hold you. Not for what you did in New Mexico, anyway.'

'There's nothing else you can hold me for.'

'The ruckus last night.'

'You'd have to hold the whole town for that.'

'You killed a man – with a shot-gun.'

'I was protecting a lady.'

'Quite a one for protecting the ladies aren't you, Mack? It seems that they've served your purpose too.'

'Keep 'em out of it.'

'All right. Now we come to the killing of Luke Piercy.'

'You can't pin that on me.'

Maginnis smiled genly. 'No, Mack, you're right – we can't. We've already got the one who did it.

As, at last, Johnson's face revealed a little interest, the marshal went on. 'It was *The Golden Hall*'s barman, the relief man, the moon-faced cuss who nobody takes much notice of, the one who calls himself Latimer. He saw his chance I guess – he'd never had a chance like it before – he never had the guts to take such a chance before. He must have gone into the office on some pretext or other, maybe pretending to warn his boss. To Piercy he was just the dumb relief barman, the great Luke would not have suspected anything. Latimer jumped him, cut his throat, then rifled the place.

'After he'd done the job he lost his nerve. He went down to one o' the smaller joints and got drunk. He waved too much money about and talked too much.

144

Poor devil, such wealth and daring was too rich for his blood I guess. We picked him up and he babbled out a confession. He's back there in the cells now – he don't know what's going on around him.' The marshal's voice faded away. There was a second of silence then Johnson said:

'Well, now I've heard your long story – a mighty interesting one too – and you've very kindly explained to me that, despite all your suspicions, you cannot hold me for anything, I guess I'll mosey along.'

'That's quite a mouthful for you, too,' said Maginnis. He did not move as Johnson rose.

Then, as the latter turned, the marshal made a sign with his hand and, walking forward, Johnson found the door barred by Charlie. He had never taken much notice of Charlie before. Now, as he felt he ought to kill Charlie, because Charlie was in his way, he took a good look at the man. He had a face like a sick fish, and pale shifty eyes.

Boot-heels scraped behind Johnson. Oh, yes – there was Pete too! Johnson turned slowly. He looked at Pete, he looked at Maginnis. The latter said:

'Just a moment, Mack – or Chipper. There's sump'n else I have to tell you. I've had a message from my old friend, the Marshal of Cripple Creek, the place you never went to – remember? He says a bunch of tough-looking gunnies rode into town a couple of days ago. He figures they came up the pass. It seems they've been tryin' to pass themselves as lawmen. They're making very discreet enquiries about a young man – answering to your description –

who might be going by the name of Johnson. It was a mistake to use a moniker you'd used before, Mack. Kinda careless . . .'

'Was it?'

'Yeh! I don't think that bunch o' tough-looking *hombres* are lawmen at all, Mack. Do you?'

'I ain't givin' it a thought.'

'I should give it a thought if I were you.' The marshal rose to his feet.

'I'm all through telling fairy stories,' he said. 'I know who those men are an' so do you. We know they're after you. They won't find you at Cripple Creek so they'll come on to El Paso. They might be on their way right now. If they are they should be here early this afternoon. By that time I want you to be away from here. Because I can't hold you – and because, strange as it may seem, I sort of took a liking to you for a time – I'm giving you a chance. I'm no saint – I ain't stopped to think a lot about whether you deserve that chance. I guess you deserve it as much as most men in this damned corner of hell. If you get the gold it won't be any use to you. The law – or your own men – 'ull catch up with you sooner or later I guess. I just don't want any more trouble an' killing in my town. I'm giving you till noon to get out. If you don't. Well . . .' He shrugged, left his sentence unfinished.

'Thanks,' said Johnson. His voice was devoid of feeling.

He turned; Charlie moved away from the door and he passed through it. They heard his boot-heels clattering away into the distance. The marshal sat down again. He took out his gun and placed it on top of the desk and looked at it.

'I hope he gets out in time,' he said softly.

Pete said: 'Let us get the skunk right away, Steve.'

'No. Go out now. Keep your eyes an' ears open. Find out what he's doing but don't let him see you following him. And no funny business – y'understand?'

The two deputies left the office, stood outside for a moment, then split up. Pete strolled nonchalantly across the road. Charlie waited a moment then went along the boardwalk in the direction Johnson had taken.

Charlie had not gone far before he met Jesse Apgood. They stopped to chat then went into *The Spinning Wheel* together. The law and the sporting element of El Paso were becoming quite friendly of late.

Mack Johnson went into a little saloon at the end of El Paso Street. It was kept by two Mexican brothers and as yet had been left unmolested by Boss Gruber and his minions. The brother who served behind the bar looked at Johnson with suspicion but gave him the glass of tequila he ordered without comment. The lean man took it absently and carried it over to a table in the corner. The other few habitues of the bar, most of them Mexicans, eyed him covertly but he gave no sign that he had even noticed their presence. Neither did his face give any clue to the thoughts that were seething in his mind. Four times he took his glass to the bar to have it refilled. Although he did not speak, apart from

147

ordering, he did not give the impression of a man with a problem on his mind. Rather did he seem like one who had made up his mind to a bout of steady drinking.

Finally he left the place, just as steadily and silently as he had entered it. He crossed the street, then went along the boardwalk. He passed *The Spinning Wheel*, the theatre, the shattered windows and gaping doors of *The Golden Hall*, and turned into Pueblo's livery stable. The little Mexican was not there. He was probably down the street having a meal.

Johnson found his horse. The beast had been freshly-groomed and doubtless fed too: he was in fine fettle. Johnson ran his hand absently along the glossy neck and looked about him. As if making a sudden decision he strode forward to Peublo's cubby, where the fat Mexican had the saddle and stuff stashed.

The door was unlocked. Pueblo was a very careless man. Johnson flung the door open and strode in. Then he stopped dead.

Jesse Apgood sat in Pueblo's chair. At the side of him stood the two frozen-faced slickers from the Barbary Coast. All three of them had guns in their fists.

'Boss would like to see you, Mack,' said Apgood.

'Why the hardware?'

'That's in case you acted offended at Boss and didn't want to come. Boss is very keen on seeing you, Mack.'

The two gun-slickers moved in closer. 'Turn around,' said one of them.

Apgood said: 'Better do as he says, Mack. I saw him

slash a man's ear off with a gunsight once – just because the fellow didn't do as he was told.'

Johnson turned slowly. He felt his hip lighten as his gun was lifted from its holster. He did not reveal the sudden lassitude which came over him.

'Walk,' said the gun-slick.

They shepherded him through the back door of the stables and along the 'backs' to the tiny rear door of the theatre. Each of them had to stoop as they went in. They passed near the stage and the dressing-rooms and could hear the clatter-clatter of the girls rehearsing.

A few moments later they were in Boss Gruber's office and the fat man was grinning at them and behind him stood Monk and the fish-faced deputy, Charlie.

Charlie's pale eyes were alight with hate and triumph and Johnson suddenly thought how funny it was that he had been finally thrown and hog-tied by this fish-faced skunk. He knew pretty well what to expect. He had played all his cards wrong. He had lost all his chips. Right now he had no hopes of getting a single one with which to gamble.

'What do you want, Boss?' he said.

The fat man's smile broadened. 'I'll be perfectly frank with you, Mack – or should it be Chipper? I want the gold. You tell me where it is and you'll have your share the same as everybody else here. You're in no position to bargain.'

Johnson's face suddenly creased in a grin. 'No, I guess I haven't.'

'You've got nothing to grin at either. Such

unwanted levity is unusual in you, Mack.'

'A man's gotta laugh sometime.'

'You picked a queer time to laugh.' Boss sounded almost aggrieved.

Johnson began to chuckle. 'You want the gold. I know where it is. I don't tell. You kill me. Then you'll never know where the gold is.'

Boss rose suddenly. His chair went over behind him. A fold of his huge stomach bulged over the top of the desk. His fat, white sweaty face went an almost purple colour.

'Stop it,' he screamed. 'Stop that laughing. Stop him!'

Johnson whirled as they came at him from all sides. One of the gun-slicks went down from a haymaker. The other one swung an arm. Steel flashed in the light. Johnson tried to duck. The barrel of the gun hit him just above his ear. He went down and lay still.

They lifted him on to a chair and dragged the chair into the centre of the room. Boss waddled around from behind the desk. His face had again assumed its greasy pallor.

'Tie him up,' he said.

When he came to he was securely lashed to the chair, his hands behind it, his feet tied to the rungs. Boss, standing over him, looked like some grinning Eastern fetish. Jesse Apgood moved up and handed the fat man a bottle and a glass. Boss poured a totful of the liquor and put it to Johnson's lips. 'Take that, Mr Chipper,' he said. 'It'll make you feel better.'

Johnson emptied the glass. Boss put both glass and

bottle on the floor. 'Do you feel better now?'

'Yeh.'

'Do you feel like talking?'

'No.'

Boss's grin widened. He bent forward. 'Let me look at that wound?' he said. He scrutinised the fresh bleeding wound above Johnson's ear. He touched it lightly with his fingers, grinning all the while.

Johnson tried to jerk his head aside as the pressure of the sausage-like fingers suddenly increased. Boss grinned more. The fingers began to feel like red-hot bars of iron. Johnson called the fat man a vile name and jerked his head again. The grin faded; Boss balled his fist and struck savagely. A hiss of pain was torn from between Johnson's lips. His head jerked back, then flopped forward, fell forward on his chest.

Boss grunted as he bent and picked up the bottle and the glass. He filled the glass with the liquor and dashed the lot into the unconscious man's face. Then he caught hold of the man's hair and held his head up.

Johnson's eyes opened. Boss brought his face nearer, grinning again, and looked into those eyes. He said: 'There are ways and means of making people talk, Mr Chipper. You, being a sturdy Westerner, and knowing all about Indians, should realize that.'

The trussed man, blood streaming down the side of his face, did not say anything. His eyes glared defiance.

The game was being played out now. But he was no shyster.

Boss Gruber stood back and surveyed him. The

little black eyes shifted and twinkled in their pouches of fat. He seemed to be dwelling on outrages, rolling them over in his mind, rejecting them, embellishing them.

'I'm giving you one last chance,' he said. 'Tell us where the gold is. You'll get a good cut. A cut is better than none at all.'

There was no reply from the man in the chair. Boss leaned nearer.

'You'll tell us sooner or later,' he said. 'After I've been working on you for a bit you won't be able to help yourself. But by that time it may be too late for any of it to be of use to you.' He grinned. 'See what I mean?'

Still Johnson did not answer. Boss drew his hand back and hit him viciously then, as his head lolled once more, turned away from him.

He walked to his desk and struck the top of it with his clenched fist. Then he waddled around the room. His face was pink and sweaty, his eyes almost hidden. He seemed beside himself. His men moved out of his path and watched him curiously.

His perambulations brought him once more near the chair with the bound man upon it. He came up behind Johnson and slapped him across the back of the head with his open palm.

'You'll talk, Mr Chipper,' he rumbled. 'You'll talk.' He might have been speaking to himself. The sweat stood out on his forehead, glistening beneath the light. The room was airless, stifling. It was daylight outside; there were no windows or skylight to let it in and the hanging lamp burned incessantly.

Boss went around in front of Johnson and peered into his face.

'You're shamming,' he said. 'I mean business. I'll show you.'

The words echoed in Johnson's brain. He kept his eyes closed, letting his muscles go slack, calling up the last reserves of strength from the depths of his body.

Boss went across to his desk. He was mumbling to himself. He went around the desk and opened a drawer. 'I've got some somewhere,' he said. Then he gave a long-drawn 'Ah' and banged the drawer and came back round the desk. When he approached the bound man he had, in one fat hand a pair of shiny new pliers, the kind cowboys use for fence-repairing and the like.

He bent nearer to Johnson. Sweat was oozing from every pore of his huge flabby face. Johnson watched him from half-closed eyes. The fat man held the pliers within a few inches of those eyes. 'See these, Mr Chipper,' he said. 'Natty, aren't they? Did you see 'em, I say? Did you ?' He grabbed a handful of the man's hair and jerked his head back. Johnson opened his eyes and cursed him steadily and fluently. Boss grinned and let him go. 'Untie his hands,' he said. Apgood came forward and did the job. As soon as his arms were free Johnson lunged forward, reaching out for the fat man. Fear flared in Boss's eyes. He was as yellow as he looked.

'Hold him you fool!' he said.

Johnson's chair went over with a crash. He squirmed and threshed, trying to get out of the bonds which held his legs. Monk and Apgood grabbed him then, and Charlie, the deputy, had to rush forward and give them a hand.

The three of them held him. 'Hold his shoulders,' said Boss. 'Hold his arms.' He brandished the pliers and almost danced. His little dramatic scene was going a bit haywire. Finally the panting Johnson was held. His hands were brought forward for the fat man's inspection.

Boss looked at the long brown fingers, touched them gently with his own repulsive ones.

'What beautiful hands,' he crooned. 'No wonder you're fast on the draw. What a marvellous gambler you'd make. I used to have hands like that.' He stopped suddenly. Maybe he thought he should not have said that. Maybe the memory was not pleasant. Was it just his fevered imagination or could he detect a mocking light in Johnson's eyes?

He raised the pliers as if he would drive them into the prisoner's face. Then he thought better of it. He said: 'Those pretty hands would not be much use to you would they, Mr Chipper – if I drew your finger-nails out slowly one by one?'

Johnson did not say anything. Nobody said anything.

'Are you going to tell me where the gold is, Mr Chipper?'

Still Johnson did not speak. There was not a sound in the room except Boss's wheezy breathing. The fat man took hold of one of Johnson's fingers. 'Such beautiful hands,' he crooned. 'Made for speed. So fast with a gun.' He brought the pliers forward.

'God!' burst out Jesse Apgood. 'Don't do that, Boss. Don't do that to him.'

Boss looked up. His face was creased with fury.

'You want the gold, don't you? You'll want your share if we get it.'

'Yes! But make him talk some other way.'

'Make him talk some other way,' mocked the fat man. 'Make him talk, by all means – but do not offend Jesse's feelings. Hold him, Jesse.' Boss made a theatrical gesture with the pliers. He was grunting, bending once more, when the door flew open behind the three men. They all let go of Johnson.

Marshal Maginnis and Pete came in. They both held levelled guns. Simple Monk went for his gun. The marshal fired and Monk gave a choking cry and doubled up. Then all hell broke loose.

Johnson, his arms free, pulled at the chair and it fell over with a crash. His bonds were already loose from his previous attempt. One of the legs of the chair broke clean off. Boss aimed a blow at him with the pliers and missed entirely. Then Johnson's arms were wrapped around the fat man's legs and he fell with a crash which was hardly audible above the hideous din of gun-fire. Boss was rolling and kicking and moaning. Johnson tore frenziedly at his bonds and at last was free.

Boss was rising at the same time and he had a derringer in his hand. Johnson dived head-first at the fat man; the little gun went off and he felt the hot breath of the slug. Then the two of them were rolling on the floor and wrestling for the derringer.

Boss still had it and was trying to bring it up when Johnson chopped at his wrist. Boss's sausage-like fingers shot out straight. Johnson grabbed the gun.

Boss's other hand scrabbled at his face, bringing tearing pain to his raw wounds. He pushed the muzzle of the derringer against soft flesh and pressed the trigger. The report was muffled. The fat man gave a curious shuddering sigh, quivered once, then lay still.

Rising to his knees Johnson saw the deputy, Charlie, drawing a bead on his own pardner, Pete, who was sagging against the door jamb. Johnson fired. He did not wait to see Charlie fall but dived for the door. He almost fell over the body of the marshal, who had been shot in the head. Even as he ran he felt a sudden wave of sadness, an alien feeling. But he did not allow it to slow him up. He went down the corridor, through the door which led to the back of the theatre.

A slug smacked into the wall nearby. Somebody was after him: who it was he did not know. A sudden apparition appeared before him. He threw up his gun.

'Mack!'

It was Lucy, clad in a riding outfit, holding out her hands to him.

'Come on, there's a horse waiting outside.'

He could not question this new phenomenon. He could only trust to his sudden run of luck and play his hand. He followed her through the back door.

His black horse from Pueblo's stood there, saddled and waiting. Another horse stood beside it. As he mounted Lucy vaulted into the saddle of the latter. 'Come on,' she said.

'Lucy, you can't—'

'I'm coming with you!' Even as she shouted he put spurs to the beast and they were away, she racing neck and neck with him. They skirted a bunch of outhouses, slowing down in case of obstacles.

A man came out of an alley to the right of them. He saw the gun in Johnson's fist and his own hand dipped. Steel flashed in the sunlight. Johnson fired and saw the man go down. He saw Lucy's startled face then it was turned away from him. Next moment they were thundering away out of town.

'Go back, Lucy,' he said. 'Go back.'

'I'm coming with you now. Wherever you go!'

'After what you saw last night?'

'I don't care about that. I know now you had to take her up there because she saved you. I saw Apgood and the other two bring you in this morning at the point of guns – I saw them through my dressing-room door. I went and found the marshal.' He could see she was overjoyed to be telling him this – although she was breathless; and any moment the pursuit might be at their heels.

Back in town there was another rattle of gun-fire. He looked back. Finally he saw a bunch of men riding out after them.

Lucy looked back too. 'Rangers,' she said. 'That was a Ranger you shot, Mack.'

He said: 'Go back, Lucy. They might start shooting.'

'They won't. Not while I'm with you.'

'Don't be so sure.' A phrase echoed in his mind. Something the marshal had said about the ladies serving their purpose. It looked like Lucy was adamant in serving her purpose now.

He said: 'We ought to be able to beat 'em to the river. Then if we can get across . . . It's purty calm. Here – this way.' He turned his horse a little.

157

They rode parallel with the trail which led out of town. Johnson kept glancing over his shoulder. He was jubilant: it seemed like they were drawing ahead.

Then Lucy shouted. 'There's somebody coming along the trail towards us.'

He looked then. 'Keep going,' he said. 'Let's get closer so that we can see who they are. They're not to know we're being chased. Not a beautiful girl like you. Trust to luck.'

As the distance between them and the other party lessened Johnson counted four men. His heart began to sink and he knew his hand was played out: he knew he held no more aces. There was only one thing he could do.

He leaned sideways in the saddle. 'Listen, Lucy,' he said urgently. 'Listen carefully.'

Her eyes widened in surprise. 'I'm listening, Mack.'

'We've got to part now. You've got to go. These men are after me, too. We haven't much time. Listen. Devil's Pass in New Mexico, the other side of the Rio – at the other end of the pass beneath a rock shaped like a sugar-loaf they'll find the gold. If I don't get through tell the law that. I want you to have the reward. That's all – get going. Forget about me.'

'Mack! What—'

He snarled suddenly and drew his gun. 'Get going,' he shouted. 'Do what I told yuh. Forget me!'

He fired two shots past her horse's nose. The beast squealed with terror, swerved, and galloped madly away. Two shots – that left two more only in the derringer.

158

He leaned low over his horse's neck, held the gun hidden in front of him and galloped headlong for the approaching quartet of riders. He was almost upon them before they recognized him.

He heard one of them shout, 'Chipper!'

Then they were going for their guns and he drew a bead with his derringer, pressed the trigger, moved it a little, pressed the trigger again. He saw two of them topple from their saddles; then he was through the middle of them and out the other side. A giant fist smote him in the back. He jolted forward across the horse's neck and held on grimly while pain beat at him. He rode on in a nightmare while bullets whistled around him.

The ground began to slope and he knew they were approaching the Rio. The cool Rio. The waters to cool burning pain which raged in his body. With one last desperate effort he raked at the horse's flanks. Dimly he heard the splash as they hit the water. The horse lurched and he held on tightly.

He felt the water on his legs, moving slowly upwards. With it came a numbness which began to creep slowly up his body. He felt himself sinking – sinking. He knew he could not make it. He let himself fall slowly into the cool water. Finally the horse was no longer beneath him and he was floating. Then he was going down.

Before he went down for the last time he heard in the dim distance the rattle of gun-fire. A familiar sound, a fitting death-knell. The Texas Rangers had arrived.

EPILOGUE

Up in the house on the hill the girl stood by the window and looked down at El Paso and waited. She was the dark girl. The gambling girl.

Although she did not know it yet, she had gambled and lost. Down in the town another girl stood by a window and looked out. Although she had lost, too, she had won also. She knew that across the plains, in the direction in which she looked, the Rio Grande still rolled sluggishly along. It gave her a feeling of comfort to know that the man she had known as Mack Johnson was part of that river now. The river which was as lawless and untamed as he himself had been. The river which had might and gentleness, too.

As in the river so in the man.

The man and the river. The river and the man.